"What's the real reason you're here, Kit?

"Did Angela tell you I was rich? Is that why you concocted this story about the boy being mine? To cash in on it?"

As his accusation registered, Nathan saw Kit's eyes darken to an emerald green.

But Kit stood her ground. "I neither need nor want any of your money, Mr. Alexander. Whether you choose to believe it or not, I brought Mark here because I believe he is your son. But he needs a father, not a man who's bitter and angry about a past he can't change. Don't you think it's time to let go, maybe even forgive—" She broke off, sure she was championing a lost cause. "I feel sorry for you...."

"Sorry for *me?*"

"Yes. If you persist in hiding behind that wall you've built to keep everyone who cares about you away, you're going to end up a very lonely man...."

Dear Reader,

A gift from the heart, from us to you—this month's special collection of love stories, filled with the spirit of the holiday season. And what better place to find romance this time of year than UNDER THE MISTLETOE?

In *Daddy's Angel,* favorite author Annette Broadrick spins a tale full of charm and magic—and featuring FABULOUS FATHER Bret Bishop. Treetop angel Noelle St. Nichols visits this single dad and the children she's cherished from afar—and suddenly longs to trade her wings for love.

Annie and the Wise Men by Lindsay Longford is the heartwarming story of Annie Conroy and her kids, as their search for a temporary home on the holiday lands them face-to-face with a handsome young "Scrooge," Ben Jackson.

And Carla Cassidy will persuade you to believe once again that Santa Claus is not only alive and well—he's in love! Someone up above must have known that rugged Chris Kringle was just the man to make Julie Casswell smile again. Could it have been *The Littlest Matchmaker?*

More great books to look for this month include *A Precious Gift* by Jayne Addison, continuing the story of the lovable Falco family. Moyra Tarling shows us that *Christmas Wishes* really do come true in a moving story of a father reunited with his son by a spirited woman who believes in love. And there's love, laughter and merrymaking unlimited in Lauryn Chandler's *Romantics Anonymous.*

Wishing you a happy holiday and a wonderful New Year!

Anne Canadeo
Senior Editor

CHRISTMAS
WISHES
Moyra Tarling

Silhouette
ROMANCE™
Published by Silhouette Books
America's Publisher of Contemporary Romance

To my son, Craig.
This one's for you!

Happy 21st!

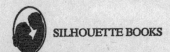 SILHOUETTE BOOKS

ISBN 0-373-08979-1

CHRISTMAS WISHES

Copyright © 1993 by Moyra Tarling

MOYRA TARLING

is the youngest of four children born and raised in Aberdeenshire, Scotland. It was there that she was first introduced to and became hooked on romance novels. After emigrating to Vancouver, Canada, Ms. Tarling met her future husband, Noel, at a party in Birch Bay—and promptly fell in love. They now have two children. Together they enjoy browsing through antique shops and auctions, looking for various items, from old gramophones to antique corkscrews and buttonhooks.

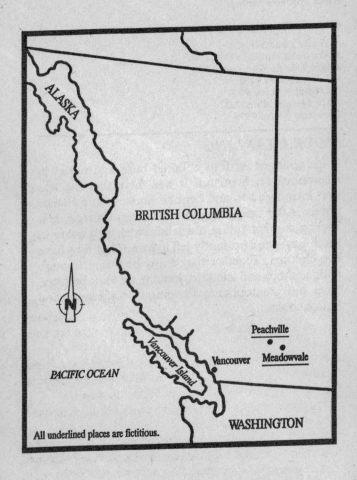

ALASKA

BRITISH COLUMBIA

N

Peachville

Vancouver Meadowvale

PACIFIC OCEAN

Vancouver Island

All underlined places are fictitious.

WASHINGTON

Chapter One

Katherine Bellamy brought the rental car she'd been driving to a halt in the snow-covered driveway of the elegant Spanish-style house located in British Columbia's Okanagan Valley.

The snow that had been falling lightly but steadily for the past fifteen minutes appeared to have stopped, at least for the time being, and it was with relief that Kit relaxed her hold on the steering wheel and shut off the car's engine.

Beside her, four-year-old Mark Vandam, her best friend Angela's son, was wriggling in his seat in eager anticipation of getting out of the car and into the snow.

"Is this where the man lives?" Mark asked as he fumbled with his seat belt.

"Yes," Kit replied and wondered not for the first time since boarding the flight from Heathrow to Vancouver two days ago, how Nathan Alexander would react when she told him who she was.

Would he order them off his property, or simply slam the door in their faces?

"Let's see if anyone's home," Kit said with quiet determination.

Just at that moment the front door of the house opened and the air was suddenly rent with the sound of dogs barking as two large German shepherds came bounding down the terraced steps toward them.

Instinctively Kit turned to Mark but he was already out of the car.

"Mark! Wait! Don't..." Kit cautioned, but the boy either didn't hear, or didn't want to hear, because he was running helter-skelter toward the dogs.

With her heart in her mouth, Kit scrambled from the car slipping on the snow as she tried to hurry after Mark.

"Cleo! Piper!" The names were spoken in a commanding tone and almost instantly the dogs skidded to a standstill, their regal heads turning in the direction of the deep, authoritative voice.

Kit followed their gaze and felt her heart slam against her rib cage as she recognized Nathan Alexander from the newspaper photograph she'd seen. Dressed in hip-hugging blue jeans and a bulky red sweater, he stood on the top step glaring down at them.

In her career as a fashion photographer Kit had met and worked with countless attractive men, but there was something about this man, something indefinable that somehow made all the other men she'd known pale in comparison.

Arrogance and self-confidence radiated from him and as Kit's glance skimmed over him, taking in his thick black hair glistening like polished onyx, his harshly chiseled features and the strong line of his jaw, she felt a shiver of apprehension chase down her spine.

"They won't hurt him," he assured her, and as if to prove his point the dogs began to wag their tails in friendly greeting as Mark reached them.

Kit released the breath she'd been holding and even managed a smile as she watched the dogs take turns licking the boy's face. Mark, whose dream was to have a dog of his own, was laughing happily, enjoying their playful antics.

"If you've come for a tour of the winery, I'm afraid we're closed for the season." The rich tones of the man's voice were much closer and Kit turned to find Nathan Alexander, the man she'd flown nine thousand miles to see, standing beside her.

Silvery blue eyes, not unlike a wolf's, locked with hers and for the second time in as many minutes Kit felt her heart stumble in reaction, and a tingling sensation the like of which she'd never felt before shimmied along her nerve endings.

She drew a deep, steadying breath. "I didn't come to tour the winery," she said and at her words a frown creased his brow.

"Then you must have made a wrong turn. Where are you heading?" he asked, his tone polite.

"We're not lost," Kit replied evenly.

"Really!" His eyes skimmed over Kit in a brief assessment that left her feeling decidedly inadequate. "If you're not lost and you didn't come to tour the winery, perhaps you'd care to enlighten me as to the reason for your visit?"

Wanting to reassure herself that Mark wasn't within earshot, Kit quickly glanced to where the dogs were still cavorting around him.

"My name is Katherine Bellamy," she announced and watched as a memory flickered briefly in his eyes. "The boy playing with the dogs is your son, Mark," she concluded with a calmness she was far from feeling.

At her words Nathan Alexander's body tensed and the expression on his handsome face became guarded and unreadable. A pulse began to throb at his jaw and his mouth curled into a tight line.

"You've got nerve. I'll say that," he said at last, his voice as cold as the December air.

"No, Mr. Alexander. You're the one with nerve," Kit was quick to respond, noting with some satisfaction the glint of surprise that came and went in his eyes.

"I beg your pardon?"

"You're the one with nerve," she repeated keeping her voice steady even though her pulse was thundering like a herd of stampeding horses across the plains. "Oh, I can understand that learning you had a son must have come as a shock to you, Mr. Alexander," she elaborated, "but to brush aside the claim without even attempting to find out whether or not there was any truth to it, is in my estimation both irresponsible and unforgivable."

Kit watched in fascination as his silvery eyes glinted dangerously. "Is that so?" he said, more than a hint of sarcasm in his voice. "Are you trying to tell me, Miss Bellamy, that you have absolute and positive proof that the child is mine?"

Nathan Alexander took a step toward her, challenge in every line of his body and Kit felt her pulse skip crazily for a moment as she fought the urge to retreat. His forthright question had caught her off guard, and the fact that he was towering over her like a jungle cat ready to pounce on his prey, added to her agitation.

Her hesitation did not go unnoticed, but before Kit could gather her scattered thoughts and answer him, Mark and the dogs came scampering to join them.

"Kit...aren't the dogs super? I think they like me," he said, smiling up at her as both animals circled Kit, sniffing at her coat with interest.

"I think you're right," Kit agreed, patting an inquisitive wet head, grateful for the timely interruption.

"Cleo, Piper, heel!" At the sharp command both dogs leapt to obey their master and in their eagerness one of them bumped against Kit, knocking her off balance and sending her stumbling into the man beside her.

His body was rock hard and unyielding and as his hands grasped her upper arms to steady her, Kit could feel their heat and their strength through the layers of her clothes.

"Sorry," she mumbled, instinctively pulling away, finding the contact strangely unsettling. Though she succeeded in freeing herself, her victory was somewhat fleeting as the shoes she wore afforded her little traction in the snowy conditions. Before she realized what was happening, her feet slid from under her.

"Oomph..." The air rushed out of her lungs rendering her momentarily dazed as she landed with a thud on the cold, wet ground.

"Kit? Are you all right?" The sharp echo of anxiety in Mark's voice brought her instantly out of her numbed state.

"I'm fine," she assured her young charge, following her words with a faint smile, silently acknowledging that the only thing bruised was her ego.

Before she could even attempt to stand up, Nathan Alexander had crouched over her, and putting one arm around her back and the other under her elbow, lifted her effortlessly off the freezing snow.

"If you hadn't been struggling like a damned fool this wouldn't have happened," he told her with obvious annoyance.

"I'm fine," she told him, deliberately ignoring the wetness seeping into her skirt and stockings. "Please, let me go," Kit said, but there was no mistaking the shaky note in her voice.

"I think you'd better come inside and dry off," Nathan suggested, ignoring her plea. "Cleo, Piper, go," he ordered the animals, and unwilling to be separated from his new friends, Mark followed the dogs.

"There's really no need," Kit told him, bothered by his take-charge attitude. The man was rude and decidedly undeserving of a son like Mark. Why on earth had she thought that turning up on his doorstep would accomplish anything? "I wouldn't want to trouble you any further, Mr. Alexander," Kit said, trying without success this time to free herself.

"In normal circumstances I'd be happy to let you leave," he responded. "But in case you don't know there's a storm moving into the area. The forecast calls for up to six inches of snow," he informed her coolly. "Your car isn't exactly equipped for these kind of winter conditions. You're lucky you made it this far. You could easily have become stranded somewhere on the road. Or maybe that was part of the plan?"

Shocked, Kit drew away from him. "Plan? I don't know what you mean," she retorted angrily. "Mark... wait!" she called after the boy, suddenly wishing she had taken the time to check on weather conditions before leaving the motel.

Glancing up at the heavy gray clouds darkening the sky Kit silently acknowledged that he was right, a major storm was definitely in the offing, and as if to emphasize the point, snowflakes the size of postage stamps began to dance their way to the ground.

A shiver chased down Kit's spine at the realization that they could indeed have become stranded in the storm.

"Shall we?" His question was more of an order than an invitation, as he urged her gently but firmly toward the terraced steps. "Besides, you didn't answer my question, Miss Bellamy. Do you have positive proof that he's my son?"

Had there been a faint ring of hope in his question, Kit wondered, or was it simply wishful thinking on her part? One thing she was sure of, however, was that she was finding Nathan Alexander's proximity infinitely disturbing.

At every point of contact with him an unfamiliar heat seemed to radiate through her body, causing her pulse to behave erratically. Much as she hated to admit it, even to herself, she was glad of his support as her legs felt uncharacteristically wobbly, a result no doubt of her fall.

"I do have proof," she said softly and at her words felt his fingers tighten momentarily on her arm.

"Nathan? What on earth is going on?"

They'd reached the front door and the question came from an attractive gray-haired woman in her seventies, dressed in a mauve wool skirt and matching sweater. She was gazing at Mark in bewilderment. "The dogs came running in first, then this little boy.... Oh...hello!" She stopped abruptly when she noticed Kit.

"Mother, meet Katherine Bellamy. Miss Bellamy, this is my mother, Joyce Alexander," Nathan said as he released his hold on Kit and closed the front door behind them, before brushing snow from his shoulders and hair.

"Don't forget me. I'm Mark," said the boy moving to stand next to Kit.

"Hello, Mark," Nathan's mother said, smiling down at the child.

"It looks like Miss Bellamy and her young friend will be staying with us for a while, at least until the storm blows over," Nathan said.

"Are we really staying, Kit?" Mark was quick to ask, his eyes alight with anticipation, no doubt at the thought of spending more time with the dogs who were not in evidence.

"I...well, yes." Kit felt her face grow warm, all too aware of Nathan Alexander's mocking stare.

"Of course, you must stay, my dear." Joyce Alexander came to Kit's rescue. "These winter storms blow in quickly and often without warning," she went on. "It's fortunate you made it this far."

"Yes, I suppose it is," Kit replied, deliberately avoiding Nathan's gaze, warmed by his mother's open friendliness.

"Mother, Miss Bellamy slipped getting out of her car and fell in the snow," Nathan said. "She'd probably like to get out of her wet things..."

"You didn't hurt yourself, did you?" his mother asked, concern in her voice.

"Just my ego," Kit said with a rueful smile. "But, please, there's really no need..."

"But you're wet, and it isn't good to sit around in wet clothes," came the older woman's reply. "Nathan, why don't you take the boy into the kitchen and make him some hot chocolate." She stopped and turned to Mark. "You like hot chocolate, don't you, child?" she asked him.

Mark nodded vigorously. "Do you know where the dogs are? When I got here they'd disappeared," he told her.

Nathan's mother smiled. "I take it you're fond of dogs," she said.

Again Mark nodded. "Kit says I can have a dog of my very own one day. I want a black lab, I like them the best," he told her. "But your dogs are nice, too," he was quick to add.

Joyce Alexander chuckled. "Most of the time," she agreed. "The kitchen's just down the hall." She pointed across the foyer. "While you reacquaint yourself with the dogs, your mother and I . . ."

"Oh, Kit's not my mother." Mark was quick to correct the older woman. "My mother died," he told her, his tone suddenly serious as well as sad.

"My dear child, I'm so sorry," said Joyce Alexander, distress evident in her voice and on her face.

"Kit's my guard," Mark went on as he slid his hand into Kit's in an action that tugged at her heartstrings.

"Guard?" Nathan queried.

Kit lifted her eyes to meet his and instantly the air seemed to crackle with tension. "I'm his legal guardian," she explained, noticing the glint of surprise in the depths of his silvery blue eyes at her announcement.

Nathan opened his mouth to comment, but before he could speak the dogs reappeared, and the tension vibrating in the air quickly evaporated.

Mark's expression immediately brightened and he released Kit's hand to pat the nearest dog, his sadness forgotten.

"Into the kitchen, you two." Nathan issued the order and tails still wagging the dogs trotted off down the hall, with Mark in tow.

"If you'd like to come with me, my dear," Nathan's mother suggested, moving off toward the stairs.

Kit hesitated for a moment. Glancing at the man beside her she noted the thoughtful expression on his face and noticed, too, another emotion she couldn't decipher flash briefly across his features as he watched Mark scurry after the dogs.

As she began to move away his hand came up to grasp her arm stopping her in midstride. He leaned toward her until his face was only inches from her own. "This matter is between you and me," he said softly. "I would advise you not to upset my mother by telling her lies." Though the words were barely audible, Kit heard the hint of a threat in his voice.

Anger rippled through her and as she shook off his hand she met his gaze head-on, refusing to feel intimidated, trying with difficulty to ignore the way her heart had once again picked up speed in response to his nearness. "I have no intention of upsetting your mother," she told him, managing to keep her voice low. "Besides, you're the one depriving her of her grandchild, not me," she concluded in a harsh whisper before striding across the tiled foyer.

As Kit caught up with her hostess who was already partway up the stairs, she knew by the telltale prickle at the back of her neck that Nathan still hadn't moved, that he was silently watching her.

While she'd expected him to deny that Mark was his child, she hadn't been prepared for his animosity. Yet just a moment ago, beneath the anger and arrogance, she'd glimpsed another emotion, an emotion he'd quickly controlled. It might mean nothing, she told herself rationally, but then again...

"The bathroom's the first door on the left," Joyce Alexander said as they reached the landing and headed down the carpeted hallway. "Slip out of those wet things... Kit... and I'll see if there isn't something in my daughter-in-law's closet that you can wear in the meantime," she added before continuing on her way.

With the words daughter-in-law ringing in her ears Kit entered the spacious bathroom. Of course! How stupid of her not to have even considered the fact that Nathan Alexander might have remarried. Angela had made no mention of divorce, no doubt believing herself to be still married to Mark's father. But that didn't mean he couldn't have divorced her.

Finding out he had a child from a previous marriage would undoubtedly have an effect on his relationship with his new wife and would go a long way to explain his unfriendly attitude, not to mention his rude behavior.

But when the opportunity to hop on a plane from London to Vancouver and drive the remaining miles to confront the man who was Mark's father had presented itself, Kit had been hard-pressed to turn it down.

In fact she'd seen it as the only choice open to her after his reply to the letter she'd sent notifying him of Angela's death and informing him he had a four-and-a-half-year-old son.

A few lines in length, his letter had simply stated that while he had been married to Angela Vandam, he was not the father of her child.

Kit, herself, had only learned the story of her friend's marriage to Nathan Alexander a few days prior to Angela's death, which had come as a result of injuries she'd suffered in a car accident.

It was as Angela lay dying that she told Kit the identity of the man who was Mark's father. Though she'd named Kit as the boy's guardian in a document of several years standing, she'd begged her friend to contact Nathan Alexander and tell him of his son's existence.

Angela had known she was dying and Kit felt sure part of the reason for her friend's impassioned plea that Kit try to unite the boy with his biological father stemmed from the realization that she'd been cruel to deny the child the chance to know his father.

Fighting back tears, Kit had made the promise that she would do everything in her power to fulfill her friend's last request.

They had, after all, been friends for more than eight years, ever since they'd met in the studios of Genesis Photography in the center of London's fashion industry.

Kit had been barely eighteen when she'd started work as girl Friday and general assistant to the three photographers who owned and ran the studio.

At nineteen, Angela had had five years experience in modeling, and had gone out of her way to help and encourage Kit that first day.

During the next few years as Kit gradually learned the ins and outs of working in the world of high-fashion photography, she and Angela had met on numerous occasions on different assignments and as a result the girls had developed a friendship.

When Kit's grandmother died of heart failure after being hospitalized with double pneumonia, Angela had been the one who insisted that Kit move in and share her flat in London.

The arrangement had worked well until Angela had been offered a modeling job in America, with the possibility of additional work once she got to New York. Angela vowed she'd keep in touch, but several months passed before Kit received a postcard from her friend.

On one side of the postcard had been a picture of the Empire State Building and on the other two short lines telling Kit that the job in New York had been wonderful and that now she was heading to California to try her luck.

Several more postcards arrived with messages equally as brief, but none bearing a return address. It wasn't until almost a year and a half later that Kit saw Angela again when she turned up unexpectedly on the doorstep of the flat they'd once shared, a tiny five-month-old infant in her arms.

Kit had been so thrilled to see her friend that she'd simply welcomed her back no questions asked. Angela had never volunteered an explanation as to what had happened to her during those intervening months, and while Kit had often longed to ask, she'd respected her friend's privacy.

That had been four years ago.

But Angela was dead and Kit wondered if she'd been foolish to make the promise to her friend and even more foolish to think she could fulfill that promise.

A knock on the bathroom door effectively broke into Kit's troubled thoughts and she opened it to find Joyce Alexander on the other side.

"I'm sorry to take so long, my dear." She gave an apologetic smile. "Try these," she said handing Kit a royal blue dressing gown and slippers. "In the end I wasn't sure whether you were the same size as Carmen or not, so I thought a dressing gown and slippers would be best."

"Thank you, you're very kind," Kit said.

"Come downstairs when you're ready," Nathan's mother went on. "You'll find us in the kitchen," she added before turning to leave.

Kit closed the bathroom door once more and sat on the small wicker stool. She removed her wet shoes and stockings. Standing, she unzipped her skirt and stepped out of it, then removed her half-slip before spreading everything over the towel rail. They wouldn't take long to dry, she thought as she slid her arms into the dressing gown and tied the matching belt securely around her.

Carrying her shoes in one hand and her raincoat in the other Kit turned to leave, only to catch a glimpse of her reflection in the mirror above the sink. She studied her rather disheveled appearance, noticing that her hair was beginning to unfurl from the bun at the base of her neck. Her face was a little pale and there were faint circles forming under her gray-green eyes, no doubt a result of the fact that her body was still trying to adjust to the change in time zones.

With a sigh she opened the door and slowly made her way toward the stairs, wondering all the while how Mark was faring.

His mother's death had affected him deeply but the sadness was slowly beginning to ebb and the happy-go-lucky, outgoing child, the child who was always asking questions, the child who had an unquenchable thirst for knowledge was steadily reemerging.

Kit hadn't told Mark the true reason for their trip to Canada, wanting to protect him as much as possible from any additional emotional pain. Losing his mother had been traumatic enough, but telling him she was taking him to meet his father only to have that father reject him, could well scar the boy emotionally for life.

And Kit understood the sadness Mark was feeling. She knew firsthand the heart-wrenching pain of losing a parent. She had in fact suffered an even more devastating blow, losing her mother and her father in a boating accident when she was only eight years old.

The accident that had claimed their lives had happened on a lake somewhere in this valley, her parents having emigrated to Canada shortly before she was born.

Her father had been a cabinetmaker, her mother a seamstress and they'd lived in a house on the outskirts of a town called Peachville.

After their deaths, Kit had been shuffled from foster home to foster home, a victim of a bureaucratic foul-up, until finally the authorities realized that Kit had a grandmother living in England.

When she'd been reunited with her grandmother the sense of relief that she wasn't alone in the world, that she did have family, had been overwhelming and Kit knew that one of the reasons she'd made the promise to Angela, that she would do her best to unite the boy with his father, stemmed from her own personal experience.

Some of the memories of her early childhood had remained strong, and at the back of her mind she admitted to herself that part of the reason for making this trip had to do with the fact that she would be in the vicinity of the home she'd known and loved as a child.

She'd never said goodbye to her parents, had never been to the churchyard where they were buried, never been afforded the opportunity to pay her last respects to the two people who'd given her life, the two people she still loved with all her heart.

If her attempts to unite Mark with his father failed, if she deemed that Nathan Alexander was not the kind of man who could give the love and guidance the boy needed, then she would return to England with Mark and make plans for the future.

But in the meantime she hoped an opportunity to track down the house where she'd once lived might arise, allowing her the chance to close the book on her own past.

"There you are!"

Kit jumped at the sound of Nathan Alexander's voice and hurriedly blinked away the tears stinging her eyes as she carefully negotiated the remaining two steps.

"I was beginning to think you'd decided to sneak off without saying goodbye," he said.

Kit bristled at the implication in his words and steadfastly met his gaze. "While you are obviously the kind of person who can turn his back on his responsibilities, I can assure you, Mr. Alexander, I am not."

Nathan Alexander came to a halt directly in front of her and Kit felt her heart kick against her breast in startled response. That she'd succeeded in riling him was obvious by the taut line of his jaw and the glittering anger shining in the depths of his pale blue eyes.

"I'd advise you to be sure of your facts before you accuse me of behaving irresponsibly," he said in a tightly controlled voice.

Kit bravely held her ground. "But I assure you I have the facts straight," she replied. "You were married to Angela, weren't you?" she challenged.

"To my eternal regret, yes," he answered.

"And you knew she was pregnant when she left you?" Kit persisted.

"Yes, I knew she was pregnant," Nathan responded in a voice devoid of emotion.

"Then, forgive me if I don't understand..." Kit said in a puzzled tone.

"Allow me to enlighten you," Nathan continued more than a hint of bitterness in his voice. "Before she left here, Angela took great pleasure in telling me that the child she was carrying wasn't mine, that she'd already been pregnant the day I met her."

Nathan stopped abruptly, almost as if what he was saying was too painful to remember. He drew a deep breath before continuing. "It didn't take me long to realize that she'd used me, that I was just the unsuspecting sap she'd conned into marrying her."

Chapter Two

Kit stared in stunned silence at the man before her, hearing the pain, anger and despair in every syllable. Suddenly the longing to reach out and comfort him washed over her, and it was all she could do to check the crazy impulse.

But whatever he believed, it wasn't true! Angela had told Kit that she'd lied to Nathan about being pregnant when they met, lied to him about everything and all at once Kit realized the enormity of the task Angela had given her.

Nathan spun away and ran a hand through his hair, cursing under his breath as those old familiar feelings of anger and frustration rose in his throat.

He hadn't intended to enlighten Miss Katherine Bellamy in such a brutal manner, but like a tenacious terrier, she'd refused to back off, leaving him no choice.

He should have known that the past would eventually

come back to haunt him. Angela wasn't the first woman who had manipulated and lied to him. Danielle had, too.

He'd been twenty-four when he met Danielle. They'd both been attending a business college in Vancouver and had been in some of the same classes. She was bright and beautiful and fun to be with. They'd started dating but there had been times when she'd been too busy to see him, or when she'd gone off for a weekend to visit family or to spend time with a girlfriend. At least that's what she'd told him.

In actual fact she'd been enmeshed in an illicit affair with a married professor at the college and when the scandal hit the front pages of the newspapers, Nathan remembered feeling like a prize fool.

No, he hadn't reached the age of thirty-nine without making a few mistakes in judgment along the way. But none had affected him quite so profoundly as his brief marriage to Angela.

At thirty-four he'd been eager to settle down, to raise a family and Angela had assured him she had the exact same goals. He'd believed her. But what he'd thought was love had quickly fizzled and died leaving him disenchanted and disillusioned.

After the debacle his marriage had turned out to be, he'd vowed never to let a woman get close to him again.

"Angela lied to you," Kit said evenly, cutting through his jumbled thoughts.

Nathan threw back his head and laughed, an empty sound that echoed off the walls, ending almost as quickly as it began.

"Tell me something I don't know." He turned to face her, but before Kit could say more, Cleo and Piper came scampering into the foyer with Mark a few feet behind them.

"The dogs were just lying on the kitchen floor when all at once they jumped up ran out," Mark said as he came to a halt.

"They must have heard my voice," Nathan said as he bent to pat the animal nearest to him.

"Dogs are really smart. They can hear sounds we can't," Mark announced.

"You're absolutely right," Nathan responded, thinking that it would be all too easy to convince himself that this bright, outgoing child was his. A pain sharp and unexpected stabbed at his heart and resolutely he reminded himself that his entire relationship with Angela had been a lie and he refused to allow her to manipulate him again.

"Is this Piper or Cleo?" Mark asked as one of the dogs playfully nudged him.

"That's Cleo," Nathan said.

"But how can you tell?" The boy wanted to know. "They look almost the same."

"Almost," Nathan agreed. "But Cleo is a girl and Piper is a boy," their owner explained.

"Oh, I knew that," Mark said proudly. "Cleo is a girl's name and Piper has to be a boy's name," he pointed out. "But that doesn't help."

Nathan chuckled softly, amused by the child's thoughtful reasoning. Crouching down he gently ran a hand down Piper's back, receiving a look of adoration in return.

"Well, if you look here at Piper's front legs, you'll see that they're slightly darker in color than his sister's," he said continuing to stroke the dog with obvious affection. "They look like two black socks, which made me think of someone in uniform, like a soldier..."

"Or a piper," Mark quickly supplied, breaking into a wide grin as he eagerly ran to give Piper a hug.

"Exactly," Nathan said quickly rising to his feet. "Okay you two, back into the kitchen," he ordered in an authoritative tone, and with that both dogs, their tails between their legs, trotted off down the hall.

"Do they always do what you tell them?" Mark asked as he gazed up at Nathan in open admiration.

"Yes," came Nathan's succinct reply as he backed a little farther away from the boy and turned to Kit. "I assume you have luggage in the car," he went on. "If you give me your keys, I'll bring it in."

"Oh . . . yes, thank you," Kit said, annoyed with herself for feeling flustered. What had she done with the keys? She gently shook her coat listening for the telltale jingle, but to no avail. "I think, in the commotion, I must have left them in the ignition," she told him.

"Fine. Let me take those," he said, indicating her coat and shoes.

"Ah . . . thank you," Kit said, dropping her coat over his outstretched arm, but as she handed over her shoes, her fingers accidentally brushed his, sending a jolt of electricity scurrying along her nerve endings.

Startled by the disturbing contact Kit's gaze flew to meet his, but there was no answering response in the depths of his pale blue eyes.

"Kit...the kitchen's this way. Come on." Mark grabbed her hand, effectively drawing her attention away from the man nearby, and it was with a feeling of relief that she let Mark lead her away.

Joyce Alexander glanced up and smiled as they entered the spacious and colorful kitchen.

"I was beginning to think you'd gotten lost," said the older woman as she opened a cupboard door above the white ceramic sink and brought out a sun-colored coffee mug. "I made a pot of coffee. Would you like some?" she asked as she set the mug on the Wedgwood-blue counter.

"Yes, please," Kit replied.

"I poured some more hot chocolate for you, Mark," Joyce told the boy. "It's on the table."

"Thanks." Mark tugged his hand free and scooted across the room to where a circular oak table with matching chairs sat in front of a bay window.

Kit's attention was instantly drawn to the scene outside, and her mouth formed a silent O as she gazed in wonder at the beautiful snowscape.

Every tiny twig on every branch, every stem on every bush was coated with a pristine blanket of sparkling snow. No surface was left untouched as Mother Nature performed her magic, creating a wintery masterpiece.

And all the while the most enormous snowflakes Kit had ever seen, so pure and white and glinting with frost, drifted past the window to form an ever thickening carpet of snow.

Kit suddenly wished she'd brought her camera in from the car, wanting to capture forever on film the almost ethereal beauty of the scene before her.

"Isn't it charming?" Joyce commented. "I just love this time of year, with Christmas only a few weeks away, don't you?" But before Kit could answer the telephone rang. "Oh...excuse me for a moment," Joyce went on. "Help yourself to coffee. There's cream and sugar on the table," she added as she picked up the receiver on the second ring. "Hello! Oh...Carmen, I thought it might be you. Yes, it's coming down rather heavily here, too," Kit heard Joyce tell the caller.

Crossing to the counter Kit filled a mug from the coffeepot and curling her fingers around it to warm them, joined Mark who was kneeling on one of the kitchen chairs. Cleo and Piper sat like sentries facing him and Kit smiled to herself as he patted first one dog then the other.

Mark was chattering to the dogs in a low voice, obviously off in a world of his own, no doubt pretending Cleo and Piper were his.

All at once Kit's thoughts flashed to those moments in the foyer when Nathan had so patiently explained to Mark how Piper had gotten his name. That he liked children was clear, but the moment Mark had moved to hug the dog, Nathan had immediately withdrawn, deftly removing himself both physically and emotionally from contact with the child.

But somehow Kit couldn't really blame him for pulling away, not after he'd told her how Angela had so cruelly denounced him as the father of her child.

Kit frowned. Her knowledge of Angela's relationship with Nathan was at best sketchy and while she had known Angela could at times be both self-centered and manipulative, she had also known that beneath the confident and often abrasive outer shell her friend liked to show to the world, there had lurked a lonely young woman.

Kit remembered all too clearly those pain-filled days prior to Angela's death, and how her friend had rambled on, often incoherently, about Nathan.

What had come across so strongly at the time had been Angela's urgent and overwhelming desire to set the record straight. But when Kit had agreed to Angela's impassioned plea to try to unite the boy with his father, she hadn't expected to find herself tossed into the center of such an emotional maelstrom.

"I'm sorry about that." Joyce Alexander's voice cut through Kit's musings, bringing her back to the present.

"No problem," Kit responded as she took a sip of the now lukewarm coffee.

"Who was that on the phone? Carmen?" The question came from Nathan who'd reentered the kitchen.

"Yes," his mother relied. "She called to say she won't be home tonight. The road out of Meadowvale has been closed. The police have been issuing bulletins on the radio all afternoon asking motorists not to venture out unless it's an emergency."

Kit met Nathan's mocking stare. "Wise move," he commented, and Kit tightened her grip on the mug she was holding, tempted for a moment to toss the contents at him. She had turned the car radio on, at least for a little while, but she'd tired of the music being played and so she'd switched it off.

"My dear, I didn't think to ask before," Joyce said turning to Kit. "Are you expected somewhere? Is there anyone you'd like to call?"

"No, thank you, there's no one," Kit said. "We're on holiday," she explained.

"Ah...heading for the ski slopes, are you?" asked Joyce Alexander.

"Well...no, we're just touring around," Kit replied.

"Oh, I see," said the older woman, though it was obvious that she didn't see at all.

"Surely you can tell by Miss Bellamy's charming accent that she and the boy are from England, Mother," Nathan said.

"Yes, I thought perhaps they were," Joyce admitted. "We don't generally see too many tourists, especially not at this time of year," she commented.

"Whatever Miss Bellamy's reason for choosing to visit our beautiful province, Mother, I really don't see that it's any of our business," Nathan was quick to point out.

Kit instantly noted the puzzled glance Joyce Alexander threw her son. She guessed he was simply trying to prevent his mother from asking questions, but Kit couldn't help feeling annoyed at his rudeness.

"Actually I did have an ulterior motive for coming to British Columbia," Kit said and at her words Nathan's head swiveled in her direction, his eyes glinting at her in warning.

"You did?" Joyce replied her expression filled with curiosity.

"Yes. I was born here," she told them and almost smiled at the look of astonishment that came into Nathan Alexander's eyes.

"You mean in Meadowvale?" his mother asked.

"Not Meadowvale. Closer to Peachville," Kit explained. "I was eight years old when my...when I left and went to live in England," she explained. "But I'm afraid I don't know the exact location of the house."

"How interesting," Joyce said.

"Riveting," Nathan said, drawing a frowning glance from his mother.

"Oh...look! The poor tyke," Joyce crooned softly, pointing to where Mark had joined the dogs on the floor and fallen asleep between them. "He reminds me of you, Nathan, when you were that age. Why, he even looks like you," she added with a watery smile.

Kit felt her heart slam against her rib cage in startled response to Joyce's innocent comment. Her gaze flew to meet Nathan's, curious to see his reaction, but disappointment shimmied through her when she found herself staring at the back of his head.

"It seems like yesterday that Nathan and his brother Jonathan were Mark's age. They spent every waking moment with the dogs." Joyce continued to reminisce. "Not these dogs, of course. We had Magic and Smoky then."

"Shouldn't we put him to bed?" Nathan asked brusquely and Kit heard the hint of tension and something more in his deep resonant voice.

"We're both still trying to adjust to the different time zone," Kit said as she set her coffee mug on the table. "It's midnight in England right now," she added after glancing at the digital clock on the microwave oven on the counter.

"Then it's no wonder the child is out for the count," Joyce said.

Kit moved around the table trying not to step on the dogs who appeared totally unconcerned about the boy's presence.

"Let Nathan carry him upstairs for you," Joyce offered.

"I can manage," Kit said, sensing Nathan wouldn't be too pleased at having his services volunteered for him.

"Nonsense, my dear," Joyce responded. "Besides those slippers look too big for you, you might trip on the stairs and fall."

Kit had little option but to graciously bow to her hostess' suggestion. She threw an apologetic smile at Nathan as she stepped out of his way, but he studiously ignored her as he crouched beside the boy. In a movement that seemed effortless he lifted the sleeping child into his arms.

"Which room, Mother?" Nathan asked as he wound his way through the kitchen.

"Jonathan's old bedroom," she said without hesitation. "Kit can have the adjoining room, that way she can keep an eye on the boy."

Mark mumbled softly in his sleep before snuggling against Nathan's broad chest and Kit noted the way Nathan's body stiffened in reaction.

"This is very kind of you. . . ." Kit began.

"Believe me, it's our pleasure," Joyce assured her with a smile. "It's been a long time since we've had a youngster around the place," she went on, a regretful note in her voice. "On you go and come down again when you've settled the boy."

"Thank you," Kit said before she followed Nathan from the room.

"I brought everything in from the car." Nathan nodded to where two midsize suitcases, and a smaller matching case, a child's backpack and a good size camera bag sat at the foot of the stairs.

Kit picked up one small case and slung her camera bag over her shoulder managing to keep up with Nathan as he continued on up the stairs.

He said nothing as he walked down the hallway past the bathroom and into the first room beyond. The bedroom, painted in a pale shade of yellow, was almost as big as the living room of her apartment back in London.

A bookshelf sat under the window and a tall dresser stood nearby. A single bed with a navy-and-white-checkered bedspread stood against the wall on the right and directly opposite was a door, which she guessed led to the adjoining room.

Crossing to the single bed, Nathan gently placed the still sleeping child on top of the bedspread.

"How long will he sleep?" Nathan asked as he turned to Kit.

A ripple of annoyance chased through Kit. "Look! His name is Mark, and while I realize this is rather an awkward situation, I'd appreciate it if you'd take your animosity out on me and not Mark. He is the innocent victim in all this."

Nathan stared at Kit for a long moment and though she wasn't entirely sure, she thought she saw a look of respect flash briefly in the depths of those incredible blue eyes.

"You're right. I'm sorry," Nathan said. "Excuse me, I'll get the rest of your things," he added and with that he strode from the room.

Kit lowered her camera bag to the floor and dropped the suitcase beside it. Tugging at the belt of the dressing gown, she wondered, after that short yet sincere apology, why she should still be angry at the man.

With a sigh she crossed to the bed and carefully removed Mark's sweater and pants before pulling the bedcovers aside, and tucking the boy beneath the blankets.

"I put the rest of your luggage in here," Nathan said when he reappeared, this time in the doorway to the adjoining room.

"Thank you," Kit said, stifling a yawn as she rose from the bed. "In answer to your question, Mark will probably sleep for an hour, maybe longer."

"Looks like you could use a nap yourself," he commented dryly, but he made no move to leave, his glance drifting to where Mark lay sleeping.

"He really is your son," Kit said softly. "Even your mother saw a resemblance," she added. "I know your wife will be upset..."

"My what?" His voice was harsh and behind her Mark stirred, and made a small sound as if he might awaken.

Kit threw a concerned glance at the boy before crossing to where Nathan stood in the doorway.

"Please..." she pleaded.

For a second he didn't move, then he retreated into the adjoining bedroom. Kit followed, quietly closing the door behind her.

"I'm sure your wife... Carmen, will accept—"

"Carmen isn't my wife." Nathan quickly cut in. "She's my sister-in-law. I'm not married. Once was quite enough, thank you," he added with a trace of bitterness.

"Oh...I'm sorry...I thought..." Kit's words trailed off and she felt somewhat foolish.

"Carmen is my brother's wife...his widow, actually," Nathan explained tiredly. "She's been living with us ever since Jonathan was killed in a car accident almost two years ago," he added, the pain of his loss lingering in his voice.

"I'm so sorry." Kit instinctively reached out to offer comfort, but when her fingers touched his, he jerked his hand away, almost as if she had scalded him.

Suddenly the air between them was crackling with tension and Kit swallowed convulsively, trying with difficulty to ignore the tingling heat skimming along her arm.

"I'm sorry," she repeated, backing away, not knowing what else to say.

Nathan's head snapped up, his eyes glowing with an emotion she couldn't decipher. "Damn it, woman! Don't keep apologizing. I neither need nor want your sympathy." He shot the words at her like bullets from a gun and it was all Kit could do to hold back the tears stinging her eyes. "You've wasted your time coming here. Angela made a fool of me once. I'm sorry about her death, but I'm not going to fall for any of her tricks again."

With that Nathan spun around and headed from the room leaving Kit staring after him in utter dismay.

Chapter Three

Kit drew a steadying breath before crossing to close the door leading into the hallway. She stood for several minutes feeling totally dejected.

That Nathan had been deeply hurt by Angela and her lies was abundantly clear, but Kit also sensed that beneath that wall of stubborn resistance was a man crying out for comfort, for love.

With a tired sigh, Kit turned and made her way into the adjoining room where Mark lay sleeping. After closing the drapes, she gently brushed a kiss on Mark's forehead before returning to her own bedroom, leaving the door ajar.

Glancing around she noticed with interest that the floral quilt atop the double bed matched the drapes and the wallpaper border. The carpet was a pale green in color and the walls a creamy shade of peach, giving an overall picture that seemed to have a soothing effect.

Kit lay down on the bed and tried to relax, but her

thoughts automatically returned to Nathan and the problem facing her.

After Angela's death Kit had taken an indefinite leave of absence from the photography studio, feeling strongly that Mark needed a safe and secure environment to work through the pain of losing his mother. Kit remembered all too clearly her own feelings of abandonment when her parents had died and she hadn't wanted Mark to have to go through a similar experience.

During the first few weeks she had diligently searched through all the papers in Angela's room, but she'd found nothing that gave credence to the things her friend had told her.

Two months later a letter addressed to Angela arrived from a local bank informing her that payment was due for renewal of a safe-deposit box. That's when Kit found what she'd been searching for.

The safe-deposit box proved to be a treasure trove. In it Kit had found Angela's marriage certificate, Mark's birth certificate, as well as a number of other papers including a newspaper clipping and photograph of Nathan Alexander with the caption mentioning his winery in British Columbia and his success as a vintner.

Though faded, the photograph captured all the intensity and intelligence of the man as well as his startling good looks. Kit had studied the picture countless times, convinced that there was a resemblance between Mark and the man Angela had sworn was his father.

And so after much soul-searching she'd penned the letter to Nathan Alexander, but it had been one of the most difficult letters she'd ever had to write.

Legally she was Mark's guardian and loving the child as she did, she was quite prepared to take on the responsibility of raising him on her own. But in light of what

Angela had told her regarding Nathan Alexander, Kit wasn't at all sure the papers she'd signed several years ago were still valid.

Tempted though she'd been to consult a lawyer, in the end she'd held her own counsel, sure that if she told the authorities about the existence of Mark's father, they would promptly remove the boy from her care and put him in a foster home until such time as they could determine what to do with him.

The thought of Mark being shunted around as she had once been was more than Kit was willing to accept or agree to and that had been another reason why she had opted to deal with the situation in her own way.

Another month had gone by before she'd received Nathan Alexander's brief but dismissive response.

Angry at what had appeared to be a callous and cruel rejection of the child who was his son, Kit had booked seats on the first available flight to Vancouver only realizing when she picked up the tickets, that the return flight was scheduled for a few days before Christmas.

Perhaps arriving on the man's doorstep in the middle of winter hadn't been the best plan, but she hadn't been thinking about whether it was convenient, or what time of year it was; she'd simply needed to take action, any action.

She'd brought with her the papers she'd found in the safe-deposit box, including Mark's birth certificate, naming Nathan Alexander as the boy's father.

Possibly he'd known when he challenged her that she wouldn't be able to produce irrefutable proof that Mark was his. She'd learned from the papers she'd found that Nathan, Angela and Mark all had the same blood type, Group O, Rh positive. And while she knew that didn't prove conclusively Nathan was the boy's father, it proved he could be.

And what Kit couldn't quite forget was the faint thread of hope she'd heard in his voice when he'd asked if she could prove Mark was his. She sensed that though Nathan Alexander might deny it, in some deep dark corner of his heart he harbored a shadow of doubt or perhaps more significantly a tiny sliver of hope.

But even if she were to convince him that Mark was his own flesh and blood, Kit wasn't about to hand the boy over as if he were a package of goods and simply walk away, not without first assuring herself that Mark was loved and wanted and that leaving him in the care of his father was best for Mark.

But if after all her efforts nothing changed, Kit also knew that she would have to make some major decisions regarding her and Mark's future.

Prior to Angela's accident, Kit had been giving serious thought to asking her two business associates to buy her out. After five years as a partner in the studio she had managed to save a substantial nest egg, and for the past year she'd been seriously exploring the idea of opening a studio of her own, a dream she'd harbored for a long time.

Though she hadn't worked for the past six months, she was still in good standing financially, and before Mark started school next autumn, Kit had already begun to make inquiries about renting a house in the country and perhaps turning one of the rooms into a studio.

Working out of the house would enable her to always be available for Mark. Moving out of central London into a smaller rural community would, she felt sure, benefit them both, but before making firm plans in that direction she'd decided to come to British Columbia and confront both Mark's past and her own.

At the moment the possibility of losing Mark seemed as unlikely as a trip to the moon, but she reminded herself of the promise she'd made to Angela to do everything she could to unite Mark with his father, and in all good conscience, she had to keep trying.

"Kit? Kit?"

At the sound of Mark's concerned and almost tearful voice Kit's eyes flew open. She wondered fleetingly how long she'd been asleep as she rose from the bed and hurried into the next room.

"I'm right here, Mark," she assured him with a smile, as she crossed to sit on the edge of the bed.

"I didn't know where you were," Mark said. "How did I get here?" he wanted to know as he sat up and glanced around the unfamiliar room.

"You fell asleep on the floor beside the dogs, and had to be carried upstairs," Kit told him.

"Did you carry me?" Mark asked.

"Are you kidding?" Kit teased. "You're much too big for me to carry," she said with a grin. "No... your...ah...Mr. Alexander carried you," she amended, surprised at the slip she'd almost made.

"Oh... where's the bathroom?" he asked pushing the blankets aside.

"Next door, that way," she told him as she stood up. "Here, put on your pants and shirt," she said as she picked them up off the bottom of the bed. "I'll find your slippers for you."

"But I have to go right now," he told her as he hopped down onto the carpet.

"Okay! You've got your socks on, so run," she told him and almost as if she'd fired a starting pistol Mark scooted off, only to come to a jarring halt in the doorway when he collided with his father.

"Ouch...what the devil!" Nathan glanced down at the partly dressed child who'd run smack into him.

"Sorry," Mark was quick to say, before dodging past Nathan and on down the hall to the bathroom.

Nathan stood staring after the boy for a long moment before turning his attention to the woman watching him from the foot of the bed. The hint of pink on Kit Bellamy's cheeks, combined with the rather sleepy look in the depths of her gray-green eyes told him she had indeed fallen asleep as he'd suspected.

But there was something infinitely appealing about her rumpled appearance that tugged strangely at his insides and as he let his glance slide over her, he was surprised to feel his pulse quicken as he silently contemplated how she would look without the robe and with her long hair flowing loosely around her shoulders.

As it was, the belt of the robe had come undone, allowing him a glimpse of her throat, as slender and white as a dove's and as cool and enticing as a glass of the finest champagne.

"Mother sent me to see if you'd fallen asleep, too." He was annoyed to find himself curbing a sudden urge to close the gap between them and taste the promise he saw on her lips. "Dinner is almost ready," he added abruptly, startled by the direction his thoughts had taken.

"I'm afraid I did fall asleep," Kit confessed, wondering at the way Nathan Alexander's pale eyes were regarding her. Under his gaze her skin felt both hot and cold and her heart began to beat erratically.

Glancing down, Kit realized that the belt of her house-coat had come undone. Heat suffused her face and with as much nonchalance as she could muster she tossed Mark's clothes onto the bed and gathered the folds of the dressing gown together, cinching the belt tight.

"I'm hungry." The comment came from Mark who'd returned from his trip to the bathroom, and whose appearance effectively cut through the tension shimmering in the air.

"Good! Dinner's almost ready," Nathan replied, glancing at the boy. "But I suggest you put some clothes on before you come downstairs." As he spoke his gaze shifted back to Kit and for a breathless moment an emotion she couldn't decipher flashed in the depths of his eyes. Then he was gone.

Kit released the breath she'd been holding and felt her heartbeat slowly return to normal. That Nathan Alexander was a devastatingly attractive man went without saying, but she found her reaction to him more than a little disturbing.

"Did you find my slippers?" Mark wanted to know, his question cutting through her wayward thoughts.

"They're in the side pocket of your small suitcase, aren't they?" she asked.

"I think so," Mark replied as he scrambled onto the bed and reached for his pants.

"Here they are," Kit said as she pulled out the slippers, made to look like bunny rabbits, from Mark's case. "I'd better get dressed, too," she went on, and dropping the slippers on the floor, returned to the adjoining bedroom.

Lifting her suitcase onto the bed, Kit unzipped the top. She chose a pair of black wool slacks and pale pink sweater and set them on the bed. Turning to the smaller case she quickly located a pair of slippers.

Divesting herself of the housecoat and her blouse, crumpled from having been slept in, Kit quickly re-dressed in the slacks and sweater. She crossed to the oak dressing table and glancing at her reflection in the large oval mirror, frowned when she saw that the bun she'd wound her hair in that morning had come undone.

With deft fingers she pulled out the remaining pins, letting the braid of silky dark brown hair fall to the mid-dle of her back. Knowing it would take too long to re-braid her hair, and unwilling to keep Nathan's mother waiting, Kit tucked the loose strands behind her ears, hoping she didn't look too untidy.

"I'm ready." Mark came running into the bedroom through the connecting door.

"Me, too," Kit replied as she finished applying a trace of lipstick. She smiled at Mark and held out her hand. "Shall we go?"

A clock began to chime somewhere in the house as Kit and Mark made their way downstairs. Outside it was still snowing, its presence creating an eerie kind of bright-ness.

"I heard six chimes," Mark said as they crossed the foyer toward the kitchen.

"Then it must be six o'clock," Kit said, quickly calcu-lating that they'd both slept almost two hours.

"Cleo! Piper!" Mark called out excitedly as he freed his hand from Kit's and ran on ahead.

Hearing their names the dogs immediately began to bark as they came running to greet Mark. What followed was a commotion as noisy as their arrival earlier that af-ternoon had been.

Kit cast a worried glance around the kitchen, fearful that Mark's exuberance might result in a harsh reprimand from his father, but to her relief Nathan was nowhere in sight. Joyce stood with her back to the sink, laughing at the antics of the threesome on the floor.

"What in the name...? Enough!" Nathan's voice boomed across the room startling everyone.

Instantly the dogs became silent and Kit held her breath as Mark, his arm around Cleo, his blue eyes twinkling with merriment, grinned engagingly up at Nathan.

For a fraction of a second Kit thought she saw an answering flicker of amusement in Nathan's silver-blue eyes, but it was gone in an instant, leaving her to wonder if she'd simply imagined it.

"Now, don't scold them, Nathan," Joyce interjected, laughter still evident in her voice. "You know how much those two dogs love to play. They just recognize a fellow playmate in Mark, and they're letting him know it."

"Are they really?" Mark asked, his eager gaze still on Nathan.

Kit felt her heart kick wildly against her breast at the look in Mark's eyes. That he'd taken a shine to Nathan was patently obvious, making Kit realize for the first time that throughout Mark's young life he'd had no father figure to look up to or emulate, no masculine influence whatsoever.

Fear suddenly clutched at her insides at the thought that Nathan, with one casual, unfeeling remark, could so easily crush the youngster's fragile ego.

"It certainly looks that way," Nathan said. "I've never seen Cleo and Piper take to anyone quite like this before," he admitted, following his words with a genuine smile.

Kit's breath caught in her throat and her vision blurred as Mark's smile widened in response. Blinking away tears Kit tried to ignore the crazy hop her pulse had taken at the sight of Nathan's smile.

Gone was the tension that seemed to be hovering just beneath the surface and in its place Kit saw a warmth, a sensitivity he obviously tried hard to hide.

Flustered, she dropped her gaze, aware that Joyce Alexander was regarding her with a puzzled expression.

"Perhaps we should eat," Joyce suggested. "I thought it might be simpler tonight if we sat at the kitchen table," she added.

"That's fine," Kit quickly assured her. "We really appreciate your hospitality," she said. "Can I do anything to help?"

"Thank you, but, no," came the reply. "Everything's ready. I just have to put the dishes on the table. I hope you like chicken."

"Chicken's our favorite," Mark announced, before Kit could reply, his words drawing a smile from Joyce.

"Perhaps we should wash our hands first, Mark," Kit suggested.

"There's a bathroom just around the corner by the back door." Joyce pointed to the left.

A few minutes later they were all seated at the oak table. Kit helped Mark cut the tender chicken breast into bite-size pieces before turning her attention to her own meal.

"Would you care for a glass of wine?" Nathan's question brought her eyes to meet his sending a shiver of awareness chasing through her. "It's a Riesling from our own cellar," he went on as he poured a glass for himself.

"No, thank you," Kit replied, suddenly feeling as if she'd already partaken of too much wine, and knowing she would need all her wits about her in order to get through the meal.

She found it more than a little disconcerting to have him sitting directly opposite her and as the meal progressed, Kit was uncomfortably aware of the fact that each time she glanced his way, he was watching her.

There was something different about the way Nathan Alexander was looking at her. It was almost as if he was trying to see inside her very soul.

"So, tell me, Kit . . . may I call you Kit?" Joyce asked, flashing her a warm smile.

"Of course," Kit replied, glad of the distraction.

"You were saying earlier that you were born in this area, around Peachville?" Joyce asked.

"Yes, on the outskirts," Kit said. "I was eight when I left, but I remember vaguely that it was a small cottage with a big garden. My mother loved to grow flowers," she added, a hint of nostalgia creeping into her voice.

"And your surname . . . ?"

"Bellamy," Kit answered. "My parents were Elizabeth and Michael Bellamy."

"May I be excused?" Mark asked politely, beginning to fidget in his seat.

"Of course, child," Joyce replied with a smile. "Perhaps you'd like to give Nathan a hand feeding the dogs?"

Cleo and Piper, who had been lying quietly on the floor throughout the meal, immediately perked up their ears.

"Wow! Could I?" Mark asked turning to where Nathan was rising from his chair, plate in hand.

"Sure," he said after the briefest of hesitations.

"Mark?" Kit interceded. "Why don't you put your plate on the counter?"

"Okay!" Mark readily agreed and hopping down from the chair, carefully complied with her request.

The dogs circled the table and stood waiting expectantly. Nathan put his plate into the sink then turned and headed toward the back door with Mark in tow.

"That was a wonderful dinner," Kit said as she pushed her chair back and stood up.

Joyce rose from the table and together they collected the remainder of the dishes and carried them to the sink.

"Nathan keeps telling me I should use the dishwasher," Joyce said as she turned on the tap. "But I can't be bothered with it. There's only the three of us, Nathan, Carmen and me, and I like washing dishes, I find it rather soothing," she added with a smile as she deftly squirted washing liquid into the sink.

"Our apartment in London doesn't have a dishwasher," Kit said as she reached for a dish towel on the counter. "Mark usually gives me a hand."

"Bellamy, Bellamy," Joyce repeated Kit's surname. "That name does seem familiar," she said as she proceeded to wash and rinse the small stack of plates.

"Really?" Kit felt her heart skip a beat. "I'm surprised at that," she remarked as she lifted another plate from the rack and wiped it dry. "It's over eighteen years since I lived here."

"Do you know the address?" Joyce asked conversationally.

"I wish I could remember," Kit confessed with an apologetic smile. In the upheaval that followed her parents' death a social worker had packed a suitcase of clothes and some toys for Kit. Everything else had somehow been disposed of or lost.

"Oh...." Joyce Alexander glanced at Kit, obviously confused.

"My parents died in a boating accident when I was eight," Kit explained. "After two months of being passed around a variety of foster homes, I was sent to England to live with my grandmother.''

Joyce turned to her, distress evident on her face. ''My dear girl. How awful for you,'' she said sincerely.

Kit felt her eyes sting with tears and she could only nod in agreement, touched by the genuine sympathy in the older woman's voice.

''I can certainly understand why you wouldn't remember,'' Joyce continued, turning once more to the dishes in the sink.

For several minutes neither woman spoke, each with their own private thoughts.

Suddenly Joyce Alexander removed her hands from the soapy water. Drying them on her apron, she turned to Kit. ''Tell me, what did your father do?'' she asked.

''He was a cabinetmaker,'' Kit replied. ''And my mother was a dressmaker. I remember sitting on the kitchen floor playing with my toys and listening to the hum of the sewing machine while she worked,'' she added.

Joyce frowned. ''I recall there being a dressmaker over Peachville way,'' she mused. ''I did my own sewing in those days, but, I wonder—'' She broke off and was silent for a few moments. ''Are you planning on trying to find the cottage while you're here?'' she asked.

''Well, yes. At least, I thought I'd check around,'' Kit replied truthfully.

''I bet I know someone who'll remember your parents,'' Joyce said, with a hint of excitement in her voice. But before she could say more, Cleo and Piper came trotting into the kitchen, followed by Mark and Nathan.

''We let the dogs out,'' Mark said. ''It's still snowing,'' he told Kit as he crossed to where the dogs were sniffing under the table in search of any crumbs that might have fallen onto the floor.

"Kit has just been telling me that she's hoping to track down the cottage in Peachville where she lived as a child," Joyce commented and at his mother's words Kit noted the skeptical look that came into Nathan's pale eyes.

"Really," he said, with an obvious lack of interest, but his mother was too preoccupied to notice.

"I was just saying I think Tobias would be the one to ask. He has such a memory for people and names," Joyce went on. "Is it this weekend or next that they get back from California?"

"It's this Saturday," Nathan said. "Why?"

"Well, I thought as Kit and Mark are stranded here for a day or two anyway, thanks to the snowstorm, they might like to stay on until the Sheridans get back," she said with a smile for Kit. "I'm sure if anyone remembers Kit's parents, Tobias will. And I wouldn't be at all surprised if he knew the cottage..."

"Mother!" Nathan's voice was sharp and tinged with impatience. "I'm sure Miss Bellamy has plans of her own..."

"Actually Mark and I don't have any set plans. I'd really like to find the cottage," Kit said evenly, knowing she was playing with fire, yet unable to forgo the opportunity being waved under her nose.

"Then that's settled," Joyce said decisively smiling first at Nathan, then at Kit.

Chapter Four

"What's settled?" Mark asked as he moved to stand beside Kit.

"You and Kit are going to stay with us for the rest of the week, maybe longer," Joyce told him with a smile.

"We are?" Mark's gaze immediately flew to Kit's for confirmation.

"Yes," Kit replied, trying to ignore the prickle of sensation scooting across her nerve endings as she became aware of another pair of eyes glaring at her angrily.

"Neato!" Mark responded enthusiastically and spinning away he ran to where the dogs lay on the floor, hugging first one then the other.

Joyce's smile widened as she watched Mark. "It's amazing how much Mark reminds me of you when you were his age, Nathan," she commented with a shake of her head as she returned to the task of washing the remaining dishes.

Kit made no reply, giving all her concentration to the job of drying the dishes, careful to avoid Nathan's gaze. She didn't need to look at him to know he disapproved of the fact that she had accepted his mother's offer to prolong their stay.

And she wasn't in the least surprised a few moments later when she heard Nathan mumble to his mother that he had some work to do.

"Work, work, work. That's all he thinks about," Joyce said in an exasperated tone, once her son had left the kitchen. "What he needs is a wife and family to take care of, then he might take time out to relax. Oh, he tells me not to worry, but I can't help it. He's stubborn and proud like his father. But if he keeps on the way he's going, he's likely to end up working himself into an early grave, the way his father did."

Kit heard both the pain and worry in Joyce Alexander's voice and wished there was something she could do or say to comfort her.

"I'm sorry, my dear." Joyce smiled ruefully as she let the water drain away and dried her hands once more. "I don't mean to unload my worries on you."

"Don't apologize," Kit quickly interceded. "But please, are you sure it's all right if Mark and I stay on ... ?" She felt a trifle guilty now that she had accepted the invitation so quickly.

"Of course it's all right," Joyce replied. "Besides, it's wonderful to have a child around the house, especially with Christmas only a few weeks away."

Kit heard the wistful tone in Joyce's voice, telling her all too clearly that Nathan's mother would indeed enjoy having young Mark around.

For a brief moment Kit was sorely tempted to explain to Joyce the real reason she'd brought Mark to this part of the world. But she kept her counsel, unwilling to create more turmoil.

Even if she managed to convince Nathan that Mark was indeed his son, she still had the difficult task of deciding if Nathan would make a suitable father for the boy, providing the love and attention Mark would need throughout his childhood and beyond.

Though Joyce had commented for a second time on the resemblance between Mark and Nathan, Nathan seemed determined to ignore the evidence.

Joyce had accused her son of being stubborn and proud, and some sixth sense told Kit that beneath all that stubbornness and pride was a man crying out for comfort, for love.

"As far as I'm concerned you and Mark are welcome to stay as long as you wish," Joyce said, bringing Kit's wayward thoughts to a halt.

"Thank you, you're very kind," Kit responded, deeply touched by the older woman's friendliness and sincerity.

"Can we play a game?" Mark's question had both women turning to look at him.

"What kind of game, child?" Joyce asked.

"Happy Families," Mark replied, grinning up at Kit. "Kit and me played it on the plane, didn't we?"

"Indeed we did," Kit repeated ruefully. She had bought Mark the card game a few days prior to their departure thinking it would be a way to keep him occupied throughout the long journey. They'd spent practically the entire flight playing the game, which consisted of accumulating all four members of a particular family and then as many families as possible.

"I don't believe I know that game," Joyce said.

"It's easy to learn," Mark assured her. "The cards are upstairs in my knapsack. That's where I keep my crayons and drawing paper, my books and all the toys Kit said I could bring with me. I can go and get them if you like."

"Good idea," Joyce said and smiled as Mark scampered off at high speed.

"Walk...don't run..." Kit called out after him but she doubted he heard. Running everywhere and most often at breakneck speed was one of Mark's favorite pastimes.

"What energy!" Joyce said as she put away the few remaining dishes. "I must say I admire you for accepting the responsibility of looking after the boy. It couldn't have been easy. May I ask what happened to his parents?"

Kit's heart gave one quick, unsteady leap. She was glad Joyce Alexander wasn't looking at her, glad to have at least a few seconds to school her features and moisten lips that were suddenly dry.

"Mark's mother died from injuries she received in a car accident," Kit said softly, aware of a pain beginning to throb somewhere inside her head.

"How tragic," Joyce murmured sympathetically. "My son Jonathan died in a similar fashion, two years ago," she added sadly, with a shake of her head. "These days everyone is in such a hurry to get where they're going. I don't understand it. I never did learn how to drive and I don't miss it one bit."

"Times have changed," Kit commented.

"Indeed they have," acknowledged Joyce. "But what about Mark's father? Was he in the car, too?"

"Ah...no..." Kit said as she tried to think of a suitable reply.

"I found them! I found them!" Mark came hurtling back into the kitchen, effectively drawing Joyce's attention away from Kit and giving her the reprieve she'd been silently praying for.

"Let me take a look at those," Joyce said, holding out her hand.

"There's Mr. Bun the baker and his family and Mr. Bones the butcher and Mr. Pots the painter...all kinds of happy families," Mark explained excitedly thrusting the small package of playing cards at Joyce. "Wanna play?" he added already climbing onto the nearest chair.

For the next hour, Kit, Joyce and Mark sat around the kitchen table playing Happy Families. Their chatter and laughter echoed through the house and as Kit watched Joyce interact with her grandson, she wished Nathan had stayed to see them together.

Kit remembered well how much her own grandmother had meant to her. The patience and love, the understanding and security, Nana, as Kit had affectionately called her, had given her had gone a long way to ease the pain of losing the people she'd loved. They'd been united in their sorrow, comforting each other through a highly emotional time, and forming a strong and lasting bond.

By refusing to accept the truth about Mark, Nathan was denying his mother the joy of being a grandparent, but he was also denying Mark an important part of his family heritage, the love of a grandparent.

"Kit! Kit, it's your turn." Mark's earnest voice cut through Kit's wayward thoughts and she quickly brought her attention back to the game in hand.

"Sorry," she mumbled. With an apologetic smile she picked then discarded Miss Cream the Milkman's daughter and instantly Mark snatched up the card.

"I won! I won!" he announced for the ninth or tenth time as he added another complete family to the four already laid out on the table. "Can we play another game?" He clapped his hands and grinned at Joyce.

Joyce shook her head in disbelief. "I don't know how you do it, child. But I think we should declare you the champion."

"Oh...he's a champion, all right," Kit replied, a hint of laughter in her voice.

Joyce began to clap her hands and Kit joined in. The dogs who had been sprawled on the floor suddenly leapt to their feet, and tails wagging rushed toward the back door. Kit's heart skipped a beat as she turned to see Nathan appear, his handsome features marred by an expression of annoyance.

"What's all the racket about?" he asked as he came further into the kitchen.

"I'm the champion," Mark announced with a grin, but there was no answering smile from Nathan.

Tension shimmered in the air for a brief moment and it was all Kit could do to hang on to her temper. They'd been having fun, that was all. Surely he hadn't forgotten how to have fun?

"I don't remember when I've laughed so hard or had so much fun," Joyce told her son, effectively dispelling the tension. "You should have stayed and joined in the game with us, Nathan," she admonished lightly.

"We could play some more." Mark was quick to make the suggestion.

"Mark, I think we've had enough for tonight," Kit quickly intervened. "Besides, it's your bedtime." She pushed back her chair and stood up.

"Aww, do I have to...?" Mark protested, but Kit threw him a cautionary glance and with a puzzled frown he lapsed into silence.

"Perhaps we can play again tomorrow," Joyce suggested and was immediately rewarded with a nod and a smile.

"Let's go, champ," Kit said deliberately moving around the table away from Nathan, who stood behind his mother's chair.

"Can I say good-night to Cleo and Piper?" Mark asked glancing down to where the dogs stood nearby.

"Of course," Joyce replied.

Mark, who'd been kneeling all the while, hopped up to stand on the chair.

"Mark, please don't stand on the chair," Kit scolded gently.

"I can jump down...see?" Mark said as he pushed himself off, an action that sent the chair toppling backward. Cleo let out a startled *yip* and scrambled out of the way.

It was only Nathan's lightning-quick reaction as he snatched the boy practically out of midair that prevented Mark from falling on top of the distressed dog.

"Hey...take it easy!" Nathan's gruff voice warned, clutching the boy tightly against his broad chest.

"I'm sorry! I didn't mean to." Mark was immediately repentant, his blue eyes filling with tears.

Kit bent to right the fallen chair then glanced at Mark who was clinging to Nathan. A ripple of shock danced through Kit at the sight of father and son, their heads so close together, their profiles matching.

The likeness between them was striking and it was with a feeling of panic that Kit turned to Joyce in time to see a bewildered expression in the older woman's eyes.

Kit hurried around the table as Nathan lowered Mark to the floor.

"Chairs are meant for sitting on, not standing on," Nathan pointed out evenly, as both dogs ran up to him.

"Yes, sir," Mark replied seriously, his lower lip quivering slightly. "Sorry, Cleo," he added as the dog nudged him.

"No damage done," Joyce said with a reassuring smile.

"I think we'll both say good-night," Kit said as she ushered Mark from the kitchen.

"Did you see how fast he was? How he caught me?" Mark asked a few moments later, a hint of awe in his tone, as they crossed to the stairs.

"Yes," Kit said as an image of Nathan's muscles rippling beneath his shirt flashed into her mind.

"I want to be big and strong like him when I grow up," Mark announced.

Kit felt her heart stumble at the boy's words. She made no reply, thinking all the while of the expression she'd seen flitting across Joyce Alexander's face.

Mark's features, though still retaining some of their babyish characteristics, were essentially the same as Nathan's: the wide forehead, the square jawline. Kit couldn't help thinking that Joyce, too, had seen the resemblance.

When Nathan's mother asked Kit about Mark's father earlier, she'd been saved from answering when the boy came rushing back into the kitchen. But after what had just happened, Kit wondered if Joyce might be more than a little curious to learn the identity of Mark's father.

Half an hour later after helping Mark unpack his clothes, Kit tucked him into bed and dropped a kiss on his forehead.

"If we're going to stay here for a few days, can we build a snowman tomorrow?" Mark asked, smiling sleepily at Kit.

"I think that could be arranged," Kit replied.

"Maybe if we asked Mr. Alexander, he would help us," Mark said and Kit heard the hint of admiration in Mark's tone.

"Maybe," Kit said noncommittally. From what Joyce had said about her son, Nathan would undoubtedly be too busy to indulge in a childish pastime such as building a snowman. But perhaps if Mark were to ask, Nathan wouldn't brush aside the boy's invitation as easily.

It would be interesting to watch how Nathan interacted with Mark in a play situation, Kit mused. And friendships had been formed over lesser things, she thought with a smile.

"Good night," Kit said softly before making her way to the adjoining room and leaving the door ajar.

She didn't feel tired, but she was reluctant to return to the kitchen, fearful of the questions Joyce might ask.

With a sigh she undressed and after putting on her nightdress, she hung up her slacks and sweater and unpacked the remainder of her clothes.

Sitting in front of the oak dressing table she began to unbraid her hair. As always she found the action infinitely soothing and as she reached for her hairbrush her thoughts drifted back to those moments when Nathan had reappeared in the kitchen.

Even as she thought of him she felt her heart pick up speed and quickly she focused on her reflection in the mirror, noticing the faint blush on her cheeks. She frowned.

What was it about the man that caused her to react like this? she wondered. It seemed that each time she saw him, each time those pale eyes of his met hers, her body responded almost of its own accord.

She couldn't recall ever experiencing such an unusual phenomenon before. Not that she'd had a great deal of experience with men. Of all the men she'd encountered during her years working as a photographer, the majority of them had been more interested in the models she had been photographing.

Few men had ever taken the time or effort to get to know her or the woman within, at least not until she met Justin Cornwall. A professional photographer from New York, Justin had come to England to work out of the studio on a free-lance basis. Kit had been assigned to assist him and she'd found his easy smile and warm friendliness infinitely appealing. A man in his mid-thirties, Justin had been handsome, charming and one of the best photographers she'd ever had the privilege to work with.

By the end of their first week together, not only had Kit learned a great deal, but she'd found herself confiding in him her dream of one day opening a portrait studio of her own.

Justin had seemed genuinely interested, offering advice and encouragement and Kit believed she'd finally found someone who took her and her work as a photographer seriously.

As a result she'd found excuses to linger after their day's work was over, asking him questions about camera angles and lighting and it wasn't long before they were spending a good deal of time together.

After his stint at the studio was over, it was Justin who suggested they continue meeting and that she bring some of her work for him to evaluate and analyze. Kit had eagerly agreed.

Sometimes during their work sessions he would casually kiss or hug her and she had regarded his actions as those of a friend and teacher, someone who not only appreciated her talents but who was both helpful and supportive. He'd lulled her into a false sense of security, gaining her trust by appearing genuinely interested in helping her further her career. But she'd had a rude and rather harsh awakening one summer evening when he'd grown tired of his game of pretense.

Kit abruptly brought her recollections to a halt and redirected her thoughts away from the past, away from the painful memory of what Justin had almost achieved. She fought back the nausea suddenly threatening to overwhelm her and gazed intently at her pale image in the mirror seeing the remnants of pain and disappointment in the depths of her eyes.

Silently she acknowledged that she'd grown to trust Justin, even fallen a little in love with him, because she'd needed to believe that she'd found one man who believed in her and her dream to one day branch out on her own.

She'd been wrong. He'd masqueraded as a kind and caring man to gain her trust, then like a poacher hiding in the weeds he'd pounced on her, revealing himself to be a self-indulgent, manipulative, two-faced rat.

Though she'd managed to make her escape unscathed, the lesson had been a painful one and as a result she'd made a silent vow to avoid any further entanglements with men and concentrate solely on pursuing her career as a photographer.

On reflection she acknowledged that the experience hadn't been a total loss. She'd learned a great deal about herself, about her own strengths and weaknesses, and she was confident that she could rise to the challenge of investing in herself by opening her own studio.

With a sigh Kit rose from the chair and tiptoed back into the adjoining room. As she gazed down at the sleeping child she wondered, not for the first time since they'd set out on their journey to British Columbia, if she had made the right decision in bringing Mark here.

She wasn't naive enough to think that once she'd introduced Nathan Alexander to his son the man would automatically accept and welcome the boy with open arms.

That Angela had hurt Nathan was patently obvious but by his refusal to entertain the possibility that Mark was his son, he showed an unwillingness to forgive, to let go of the past and move on.

He'd built a wall around his emotions, as she herself had done, but when she'd found herself responsible for Mark, responsible for his emotional and physical wellbeing, she hadn't had time to think of herself or dwell on the past.

And while it was tempting in the face of Nathan's opposition to take Mark and go back to England and forget about the promise she'd made to Angela, Kit knew that her conscience wouldn't allow her to leave without at least giving it her best shot.

With a tired sigh she returned to her own room and as she slid between the bedcovers tried not to think that she had less than two weeks to somehow bring about a miracle.

Kit woke with a start and darted a frowning glance around the darkened room, confused for a moment as to her whereabouts. As her eyes gradually became accustomed to the dimness the memory of their arrival at the Alexander Winery came rushing back.

Shoving the blankets aside Kit stood up and crossed to the adjoining door to check on Mark. He was fast asleep. She smiled to herself and turning away noticed the luminous clock on the nightstand.

Twelve-o-five. Five minutes past midnight. A quick mental calculation resulted in the realization that it was five minutes past eight in the morning in England. No doubt her inner clock was still tapped into that time zone.

The room was warm and her mouth and throat felt dry. A drink of water would alleviate the dryness, she thought. Where had she put her dressing gown? In one of the drawers?

Rummaging for it might disturb Mark. Maybe she wouldn't need it. Kit quietly opened the bedroom door and glanced down the darkened hallway. She listened for a moment for any telltale sounds, but heard nothing. Taking a deep breath she tiptoed down the carpeted hall coming to a halt at the top of the stairs.

Realizing that she'd walked past the bathroom she turned and slowly retraced her steps stopping in front of the first door. As her fingers curled around the ornate brass knob she knew instantly that this was the wrong door, that she'd made a mistake.

But before she could move the door was yanked open and Kit was unceremoniously propelled straight into Nathan Alexander's arms.

"What the...?" Nathan muttered under his breath before grasping her upper arms and holding her away from him, his pale eyes glinting at her like twin icebergs.

Kit blinked, blinded by the light from the room. She felt her heartbeat kick into overdrive and she fought to contain the feeling of panic sweeping over her.

"Please, let me go!" The words were only a harsh whisper but there was no mistaking the alarm echoing through them.

Beneath his fingers Nathan could feel her slender body trembling and as he met her gaze he was startled by the look of fear he could see in the depths of her gray-green eyes.

"Hey... take it easy," he said softly, soothingly, wanting to erase the look of vulnerability, of defenselessness that tugged strangely at his insides.

"I'm sorry..." Kit said breathlessly all the while trying to ignore the fact that he was naked to the waist and much too close. "I was looking for the bathroom," she said wondering vaguely if he could hear the thunderous roar of her heart.

"It's across the hall," he said as he relinquished his hold on her, and with that the feeling of panic began to subside.

Relieved Kit dropped her gaze only to find herself staring at the smooth, lightly tanned muscles of his naked chest.

Her breath caught in her throat and she braced herself in readiness for the panic to return. But to her astonishment she felt her pulse flutter uncontrollably and her skin tingle with anticipation as an unfamiliar ache slowly began to spread through her.

She drew a startled breath and succeeded only in bombarding her senses with his seductive masculine scent. Bewildered by the sensations coursing through her and feeling more than a little light-headed Kit closed her eyes and felt herself sway.

"What's wrong? Are you ill?" His hands came up to steady her once more but this time his touch was infinitely gentle creating a whole new array of sensations within her.

She heard the concern for her in his deep voice and as her eyes flickered open she fought to hold on to her crumbling composure. It was all she could do to formulate a reply. "I'm fine," she managed to say in a voice that was slightly unsteady. "You startled me, that's all."

Nathan held her gaze for what seemed an eternity and for a fleeting moment an emotion she couldn't decipher flashed briefly in his eyes.

"I'm sorry," she repeated and was surprised at the feelings of relief and disappointment that shimmied through her when he released her.

"Good night," he said abruptly, and before she could answer he closed the door.

Kit spun around and reached for the bathroom door. Once inside she sank gratefully onto the edge of the bathtub and waited for the world to return to normal. Her thoughts were in complete chaos, her emotions in tatters.

The image of Nathan's broad naked chest flashed into her mind. What if he'd been totally naked? The thought dropped into her mind out of the blue and she shot to her feet, her heart kicking wildly against her breastbone in reaction.

Turning on the faucet she splashed cold water on her face several times, then filled a glass and drank from it. Over the rim of the glass she studied her reflection in the mirror above the sink, surprised to see that outwardly at least, she didn't look any different.

Inside was another matter. Her heart was beating much too fast and her nervous system seemed to have short-circuited. Undoubtedly the fact that only moments before she'd been thinking about Justin was the reason behind her feelings of panic.

But overriding that was the memory of how quickly her panic had evaporated, replaced by those new and exciting sensations, sensations that still lingered beneath the surface, leaving in their wake a longing she'd never known before.

Chapter Five

Several minutes passed before Kit felt her heart rate return to normal. Gathering her skirt, half-slip and stockings from the towel rail where she'd left them to dry earlier, she quickly checked the corridor before making her way back to her room.

She slid beneath the covers and tried not to dwell on those moments when she'd found herself in Nathan's arms. Panic had kicked in as a means of self-preservation, as leftover fears from her encounter with Justin had rushed to the fore.

Like Nathan, he'd caught her completely off guard, but unlike her accidental brush with Nathan, Justin had carefully engineered his attempt at seduction, fully expecting to reap the ultimate reward for his efforts.

And Kit only had herself to blame. She'd been too caught up in the pleasure of having a photographer of Justin Cornwall's caliber take her and her work seriously, that she'd fallen for his lies.

But he'd baited the hook well, culminating his efforts with a pièce de résistance, inviting her along as his personal assistant on a photo shoot in the south of England.

She'd accepted, of course, thrilled at being afforded the opportunity of working with him again. The shoot had gone well. Indeed, Kit had done most of the work. They'd wrapped up around ten-thirty in the evening and tired but exhilarated, she'd gone to her room.

Half an hour later Justin had appeared at her door with a bottle of champagne and two glasses, inviting himself in for a celebratory drink.

Surprised but not alarmed Kit had let him in, but as she accepted a glass of champagne she quickly realized that Justin had already consumed most of the bottle's contents and had much more in mind than simply sharing a drink with her.

At first she had hoped to be able to deal with the situation with a mixture of humor and diplomacy. But Justin had had his own agenda, telling her quite callously that she was naive if she thought he'd wasted all this time on her to be denied his just rewards.

Before she'd been able to speak or react he'd hauled her into his arms, kissing her throat and neck, his hot breath fanning her face as he told her how long he'd waited and planned for this, and how much he was going to enjoy her.

A mixture of shock and fear had held Kit motionless for several agonizing moments and Justin, undoubtedly taking her inaction as acquiescence began to caress her breasts.

Disgust had Kit's skin crawling, but anger came to her rescue and with a burst of strength she broke free of his embrace, immediately bringing her knee up in the ultimate defensive motion.

Her aim proved to be perfect and as Justin crumbled to the floor writhing and moaning in agony, she'd quickly gathered her things together and walked out.

She'd never seen Justin again. But she had seen the finished photographs used in the advertising campaign...her photographs. Still, she'd considered that a small price to pay.

"Kit! Kit! Are you awake?" The quiet excitement in Mark's tone aroused Kit from the realms of sleep, and she opened her eyes to find him standing at her bedside.

"I am now," she said with a yawn. "Good morning," she added with a smile.

"You should see the snow outside," Mark said. "There's lots and lots of it," he told her, a hint of wonder in his voice.

"Enough to make a snowman?" she asked, pushing the covers aside.

"I bet there's enough to make a billion snowmen," Mark confirmed, grinning at her.

Kit laughed as she rose and crossed to open the draperies. "Oh...I think you're right," she said as she gazed out over the snowy landscape.

Once again Kit was struck by the sheer beauty of the outlying countryside. Beyond the winery itself row upon row of snow-covered vines spread across the landscape, giving the impression of an enormous patchwork quilt, while the trees scattered here and there looked like white-coated sentinels standing guard.

"There's Mr. Alexander with Cleo and Piper." Mark's comment brought Kit's attention back to the yard below, where Nathan, the dogs bounding ahead of him, had just come into view.

"I wonder where he's going," Mark said seconds before he began to knock on the window in an attempt to attract Nathan's attention.

"Mark, don't!" Kit tried to stop him, but she wasn't quick enough, as she watched Nathan turn and gaze up at them.

Realizing that she was wearing only her nightdress, Kit felt her face grow hot with embarrassment as the memory of their encounter washed over her.

Beside her Mark was waving enthusiastically at the figure below and as Kit took a step back she silently prayed Nathan would at least acknowledge the child. Her prayer was answered when Nathan lifted his hand in a brief salute before continuing on his way.

"I bet I could catch them if I hurry," Mark said, spinning away from the window.

Kit caught him in midstride. "You're not even dressed," she remarked with a shake of her head.

"Oh . . . I forgot," Mark said, glancing down at his pajamas.

"Come on sport, I'll give you a hand and by the time you wash and dress, I bet they'll be back from their walk," Kit said, in an attempt to erase his downcast expression.

"Okay," Mark replied.

Kit located her housecoat and collected the bag of toiletries from on top of the dressing table and together they headed for the bathroom.

Half an hour later Kit and Mark made their way downstairs. Mark, dressed in a fleece-lined navy sweatshirt and matching pants, scampered down the stairs ahead of Kit, eager to get to the kitchen.

Kit had also opted for casual attire and was wearing black stirrup pants and a baggy multicolored long-sleeved shirt, cinched at her waist with a wide gold belt.

As she crossed the foyer, the front door opened and amid a flurry of cold air Piper and Cleo, followed by Nathan bustled in.

Kit felt her heart skip a beat at the sight of Nathan's tall, imposing figure. His black hair was in riotous disarray and his cheeks had a healthy red glow.

"Good morning," she said, and was annoyed to hear the hint of breathlessness in her voice. "Has it stopped snowing?" she asked as she patted both dogs.

"Yes," Nathan responded as he shrugged out of his bulky red ski jacket. "Cleo! Piper! Off to the kitchen, you two," Nathan ordered and the dogs trotted off obediently.

Kit turned to follow. "Hold on a minute." Nathan's authoritative tone brought her to a halt and she turned to face him. "You and I need to have a little chat," he went on before turning to hang his jacket on the coat stand nearby, then bend down to remove his boots.

"About what?" Kit asked, firmly keeping her nerves in line as he rose to his full height once more and took a step toward her.

"That business about your parents living in Peachville, was it true?" he asked.

"Of course it's true," Kit replied, startled by the question. "Why would I lie?"

Kit watched in fascination as Nathan's mouth curled into a cynical smile. "It's been my experience that women lie simply as a means to an end, and your little story garnered sympathy and an invitation to stay on after the storm blows over," he asserted.

Kit bristled at his insinuation. "I wasn't lying. I *would* like to track down the cottage where I was born and lived with my parents," she reiterated, surprised that she should feel hurt that he'd assumed she was lying. "Your mother was very kind to make the offer. She has a warm, generous nature as well as a kind heart."

"Meaning I don't?" Nathan said, a hint of humor in his voice now.

"Well, it's easy to see that you don't take after your mother," Kit said, unwilling to back down. "I'm not even sure you have a heart..." she countered boldly.

"Really?" There was a definite challenge in his tone now, a challenge she found difficult to resist.

"Really," she replied. "In fact it's my guess your heart has probably shriveled up from all that bitterness and resentment you like to carry around with you." At her words she saw a flicker of admiration dance briefly in the depths of his pale eyes before it was replaced by an angry glitter.

"Oh, I have a heart, all right," Nathan said. "Here, see for yourself." And before Kit could think or react Nathan captured her wrist, placing her hand firmly on his broad chest.

Beneath the dark blue lambs-wool sweater he wore, Kit could feel the solid beat of his heart and immediately felt her own accelerate in response. She tried to muster up feelings of anger and indignation at his he-man tactics but when she lifted her eyes to meet his, the words of protest hovering in her throat died before they reached her lips.

They stood staring at each other like china figurines trapped in a moment of time. Kit could scarcely breathe, all too aware of the hard, lean strength of Nathan's body only inches away.

Suddenly against her palm she felt his heart pick up speed to mark time with her own and at the point of contact a strange, unfamiliar heat began to shoot along her fingers and up her arm, a heat that seemed to rob her of the will to move away.

Nathan hadn't been entirely sure just what he'd hoped to accomplish when he'd placed her hand over his heart. But whatever the reason, it had definitely backfired for he suddenly found himself fighting the urgent need to haul her close and taste the promise of sweetness her sensuous mouth was offering.

Since their brief clash upstairs the night before, he'd had difficulty chasing the image of those classic features from his mind: those high, slanting cheekbones, her long, thick eyelashes framing eyes that flashed green one minute, gray the next.

There was something indefinable about this woman, something he couldn't easily dismiss. She had an air of quiet confidence, a determination he grudgingly admired. And if the truth be told he was more than a little unnerved by her steadfast belief that Mark was his son.

But much as he might—in some secret corner of his heart—want to believe her claim, Nathan found it impossible to erase from his memory the cruel and callous way Angela had destroyed his dreams. In a voice edged with icy disdain she'd informed him that the baby she was carrying wasn't his, that she'd been pregnant when they met, and that she'd duped him into marriage for reasons he'd never been able to fathom.

Suddenly Nathan dropped Kit's hand and glancing up at him she was surprised at the look of pain that flashed fleetingly in his eyes.

"I told you I have a heart," he said evenly. "And to further prove my point I'm willing to offer a truce. My mother appears to have taken a shine to you and the boy and if it makes her happy to have you here then I'll go along with that . . . for the time being. But let me give you this word of warning." His tone sent a shiver chasing through her. "I'll be watching you like a hawk and if you mention your connection to Angela, or if you try to manipulate my mother or take advantage of her in any way, shape or form, I will personally escort you and the boy out of this house and off my land. Do I make myself clear?"

"Perfectly," Kit said. Whatever she'd expected him to say, suggesting a temporary truce had not even been on her list and it was all she could do to contain the feeling of elation sweeping through her.

"Then we understand each other," he said before moving past her toward the stairs.

"Absolutely," said Kit, thinking that in some strange way Nathan had passed the first test. He'd just proved that he was a reasonable man, willing if only for his mother's sake to put aside his animosity and offer a compromise.

Kit stood staring after him as he took the stairs two at a time. Slowly she released the breath she hadn't known she'd been holding. She still couldn't quite believe what had happened but she wasn't about to argue the outcome. It was definitely a beginning.

It was apparent from his comments that Nathan considered her to be a woman just like Angela, a woman willing to lie to get what she wanted, and Kit was surprised that she should feel hurt, that she should care what he thought of her.

She had always prided herself in being an open and honest person, learning at a young age that lies only led to more lies and inevitably the lies became so tangled and distorted the only way out was to tell the truth.

Kit knew that Nathan's distrust had to have stemmed from his experience with Angela, but deep down in her heart Kit firmly believed that Nathan needed the boy in his life as much as Mark needed a father.

Somehow she had to help Nathan regain the trust he'd lost, break down the barriers he'd erected to keep from being hurt again. But Mark's happiness and well-being were also at stake here and although Nathan didn't know it, he still had a long way to go to prove that he was worthy of a son like Mark... worthy of the title of father.

With a sigh Kit made her way to the kitchen where she found Joyce and Mark and the dogs. The tantalizing aroma of bacon cooking filled the air making Kit's mouth water and she was relieved that Mark, busy with the dogs, made no comment about her tardiness.

"Good morning, Kit," Joyce greeted her with a warm smile. "Did you sleep well?"

"Yes, thank you," Kit replied. "Is there anything I can do to help?"

"Well... if you're sure..." Joyce began as she slid her hand into an oven glove.

"Please, I'd really like to help," Kit assured her hostess. "You've been more than kind to extend your hospitality this way... to strangers, I mean."

"You're more than welcome, my dear," Joyce replied. "Besides, since you grew up right here in B.C. you're not really a stranger. And it's such a joy to have a youngster around the house again. Children have a way of making Christmas so special," she said as she carried the plate of bacon to the table. "I had thought at my age to have a few grandchildren of my own by now," she went on. "So forgive me for being a little selfish in wanting you and Mark to stay," she finished with a teary smile.

Kit's heart ached for the woman beside her and somehow she felt justified in some small way for bringing Mark to Canada if for no other reason than to afford Joyce the opportunity of spending time with her own grandchild.

"Shall I set the table?" Kit asked.

"That would be lovely," Joyce said. "The place mats and cutlery are in the top two drawers. There's a platter of pancakes keeping warm in the oven. I wonder... did Nathan go upstairs?"

"Yes, he did," Kit answered as she arranged forks and knives around the table.

"I'll find him," Mark said hopping to his feet.

"Find who?"

Kit almost dropped the fork in her hand at the sound of Nathan's deep voice.

"There you are, Nathan. Your timing is perfect. Breakfast is ready. Pour yourself a cup of coffee and sit down," his mother instructed.

"Mark, go and wash your hands, please," Kit said as she finished setting the table, and Mark nodded and hurried off to the nearby bathroom.

"So, Kit, tell me, what type of work do you do in England?" Joyce asked once they were all seated at the table.

"I'm a photographer," she said. "At least I was," she amended.

"Really! How interesting," the older woman commented.

"I'm hoping to open my own studio when I get back," Kit said, all the while aware that Nathan was listening intently to every word.

"In London?" Joyce asked.

"No, actually I've been thinking about looking for a place somewhere in the country," she said.

"That sounds like quite an undertaking, financially and emotionally," Nathan said.

"Yes, I suppose it will be," Kit responded easily, determined not to elaborate further. After all, what she did when she returned to England was none of his business.

"How did you become interested in photography?" Nathan asked.

Kit met his gaze across the table and was surprised at the look of genuine interest she could see in his eyes.

"Taking pictures has always been a hobby of mine, ever since my grandmother gave me a camera for my tenth birthday," Kit said smiling fondly at the memory. "When I left school and went up to London to find a job, I was lucky enough get work in a small studio. I was their girl Friday at first, then gradually worked my way up to assistant photographer. These pancakes are delicious," she said, smiling now at Joyce.

"Thank you," Joyce said. "I wish you every success with your venture, my dear. Oh...Nathan, what are your plans for this morning?"

"Why? Is there something you want me to do?"

"Well . . . no," she replied.

"Me and Kit are going to build a snowman," Mark said, his eyes sparkling with excitement. "Want to help us?"

Kit kept her eyes on her plate and held her breath as she waited for Nathan to answer. The silence, though it lasted only a few seconds, seemed interminable.

"I'm afraid I have work to do," Nathan said at last and Kit glanced up in time to see the look of disappointment on Mark's face.

"What do you have to do?" the boy asked, not one to give up easily.

Nathan shifted in his chair, throwing Kit a frowning glance. "I have a number of things at the winery that need my attention," he said noncommittally.

"What kind of things?" Mark asked.

Kit reached for her coffee cup, careful to avoid Nathan's gaze, aware of his growing discomfort, but she refused to bail him out, wanting to see just how he would handle Mark's persistent questioning.

"I have a list of things to do each day, a routine that I follow every morning," Nathan explained.

"And how long does it take to do the list?" Mark wanted to know.

Kit tried hard not to smile. She knew firsthand that Mark was attempting to wear Nathan down. It was a tactic he'd used successfully on her countless times whenever he wanted her to spend time with him.

"Most of the morning, probably," Nathan replied, and to his credit Kit noted that there was no hint of impatience in his voice.

"We can wait until you're finished your 'rooting' and then you could help us build a snowman," Mark said, moving in for the kill.

At Mark's words a smile flickered across Nathan's features only to be quickly controlled. "Actually I don't..." Nathan began.

"Nathan..." Joyce reprimanded gently. "Surely you can take an hour out of your day and help the boy build a snowman. It'll do you good. You spend far too much time checking and rechecking everything. What was the point of putting in all that automated equipment last year if you're still going to continue to hover over it like a mother hen?"

"I concede," Nathan said, with evident amusement in his voice. "After lunch I'll help you build a snowman." He accepted his defeat with good grace.

"Neato!" Mark said, immediately brightening at the prospect of having Nathan's help after all. "We'll make the biggest snowman in the whole world."

"Now that wasn't so difficult, was it?" Joyce commented.

Nathan merely shook his head. "No, but I think I'll go and get some work done before I get railroaded into doing something else."

"Why don't you take Kit along with you, give her a guided tour of the winery," Joyce suggested.

Kit almost swallowed her tongue. "Thank you, Mrs. Alexander, but that's not necessary," she managed to say. "Besides, I can't leave Mark on his own..."

"I'll be here," Joyce was quick to point out. "I was planning on getting some of my Christmas baking done this morning. I thought Mark might like to give me a hand. What do you say, Mark?"

"Okay," the boy replied as he popped the last sliver of pancake into his mouth.

"I'll give Kit a tour another time," Nathan suggested.

"No problem." Kit quickly jumped in before Joyce decided to insist.

"If you'll kindly excuse me," Nathan said, rising from the chair, an action that brought the dogs instantly to their feet.

"Are you taking Cleo and Piper with you?" Mark asked as he watched the animals move to where Nathan stood.

"They like to keep me company," Nathan replied as he carried his plate to the sink.

Joyce rose and began to gather the plates from the table. "You really like dogs, don't you, Mark?" she said.

Mark nodded his head vigorously. "I wrote Santa a letter asking him to bring me a puppy for Christmas," he told her. "I even drew him a picture," he added proudly.

Kit felt a hand clutch at her heart at Mark's words. She glanced at Nathan surprised to see a glimmer of some emotion, understanding perhaps, dance in the depths of his eyes.

"Santa must be very busy these days reading letters from children," Nathan said, the barest hint of a smile curling at his mouth.

"I mailed my letter ages ago just to make sure he'd get it in time," Mark said. "There's only thirteen days left till Christmas. I can hardly wait," he added with a confident smile.

Kit caught the questioning glance Nathan threw her way and she answered with an imperceptible shake of her head. Much as she wanted to fulfill Mark's Christmas wish, she'd decided that it would be foolish to acquire a puppy until she was more certain about the future.

"We've always had dogs around this house," Joyce said. "I remember the Christmas Nathan asked Santa for a puppy," she said, her tone full of happy reminiscence.

"Did your Christmas wish come true? Was there a puppy under the tree on Christmas morning?" Mark asked, eagerly turning to Nathan.

"Yes, there was," said Nathan, his smile widening at the memory.

Kit felt her heart kick wildly against her breast as his smile took her breath away.

"Neato!" Mark said excitedly.

"Are you spending Christmas in Canada?" Joyce asked.

"No, we leave Vancouver on the twenty-second," Kit answered, thinking all the while that if things didn't work out, Christmas would be a rather sad affair for Mark, especially if there was no puppy under the tree.

Silently Kit made a vow that if Mark returned to England with her she would do her utmost to get him the puppy he yearned for just as soon as she found a house in the country.

"I've even picked a name for my puppy." Mark's voice cut through Kit's wayward thoughts. "I'm going to call him Sooty 'cause he's gonna get covered in soot when Santa comes down the chimney with him," he added with a wide grin.

Nathan laughed, a spontaneous burst of sound startling everyone, including Nathan himself. His glance flew to meet Kit's and she watched as his expression swiftly changed, his smile vanishing, as if he'd been caught fraternizing with the enemy.

"Sooty is a great name," Nathan said abruptly. "Now I really must go. Cleo, Piper... come." At his command the dogs obediently ran to his side, following their master from the kitchen.

"It's been so long since I heard him laugh like that," Joyce said in a wistful voice. "I wish he'd do it more often."

Kit rose and carried her plate to the sink thinking of those moments when Nathan had allowed a warmer, friendlier side of his personality to emerge.

The change had been dramatic, showing a side of him she could easily grow to like, a side he seemed determined to keep hidden.

Joyce had voiced a wish that her son would laugh more often, and Kit suddenly found herself making a wish of her own. After all, wasn't this the season for miracles, the season when wishes—especially Christmas wishes—were supposed to come true?

Chapter Six

"Let's bake cookies, shall we?" Joyce said in a cheery tone.

"What kind of cookies?" Mark asked.

"Christmas cookies, of course, and tarts, too, maybe. If you look in the bottom of that cupboard you'll find a container with cookie cutters," Joyce told him. "Pick out all the ones with Christmas designs and we'll rinse them off."

"I'll wash these dishes," Kit offered, moving toward the sink.

"Don't worry about those," Joyce suggested. "We can do them all together when we're finished."

The remainder of the morning flew by in a flash. The aromas of cinnamon and cloves permeating the air added a definite festive quality to the kitchen and Kit smiled to herself as she watched Mark with his grandmother.

Joyce gave the boy free rein yet still managed to maintain order as Mark, with dabs of flour on practically every area of his anatomy that wasn't covered, applied himself energetically to each and every task. Mark enjoyed himself immensely as he helped mix flour and sugar, add spices and other essential ingredients under Joyce's supervision.

Throughout the lesson Joyce kept a running conversation, relating stories about Nathan and his brother when they were children and in with the memories Kit heard sadness amid the laughter.

Kit filled the sink and washed dishes, watching as Joyce, with endless patience, encouraged Mark to roll out the cookie dough by himself. And later she held his small hand steady while he pressed down on the cutters to form the trees and angels and stars, the shapes he'd chosen.

With each smile and helpful word Joyce charmed her way into the boy's heart and when the cookies and tarts were at last completed and out of the oven, Mark helped arrange his work on cooling trays.

Kit knew by the wide smile and look of pride on Mark's face that it would be a long time before he would forget this special morning.

"Can we do this again tomorrow?" Mark asked as he finished decorating the cookie trees with red and green colored candied fruit.

Joyce laughed. "Well, I suppose we could make another batch of cookies to take with us to the Sheridans'," she said.

"What's the Sherdans?" Mark promptly asked.

"Not what, who." Joyce replied. "Vienna and Drew Sheridan—" she carefully pronounced the names "—are friends of ours and they have two children. Chris is ten now, and his little brother Kade is almost two. Vienna is the local vet," she explained.

Mark's eyes widened with interest. "Doesn't a vet look after animals when they get sick?" He turned to Kit for confirmation.

"That's right," she replied.

"I want to be a vet when I grow up," Mark announced. "Then I can have all the dogs I want. Are we going to the...Sheridans', too?" he asked, careful to say the name properly this time.

"Yes, Kit wants to talk to the boys' grandfather," said Joyce. "You'll be able to meet Chris and Kade and their dogs...speaking of dogs," she hurried on as she dried the last of the cookie trays. "I hear Cleo and Piper at the back door, they must have got tired of waiting for Nathan."

"I'll let them in," Mark said eagerly, hopping down from the chair he'd been kneeling on.

As Mark ran to the back door, Joyce glanced at the digital clock on the microwave oven. "It's almost lunchtime," she said. "Kit, would you walk down to the buildings and tell Nathan lunch is ready? By the time you get back I'll have warmed up the pot of soup I made yesterday, and thrown together a few tuna sandwiches."

"Are you sure we should disturb him?" Kit asked, more than a little reluctant to visit the lion in his den.

"Of course," Joyce replied. "Besides, he promised Mark he'd help him make a snowman, didn't he? You can't miss the office. Just cross the patio then follow the path until you come to the main building. Go in and Nathan's office is the first on the right."

A few minutes later Kit, wearing a coat and boots that belonged to Joyce's daughter-in-law, Carmen, made her way across the snow-covered patio and down the path leading to the building. The temperature outside was below the freezing mark and Kit was thankful for the warm clothing Joyce had loaned her.

Kit smiled to herself as she thought about the morning's activities and how Joyce had reminded her of her own grandmother, and the many happy times they'd had together. If she'd had to handpick someone for the role of Mark's grandmother Joyce would have been an obvious choice, fitting the requirements to a T.

Listening to Joyce relate stories about Nathan and his brother as children, Kit had heard the warmth and the love in her voice and wondered, not for the first time, if the son she'd spoken so lovingly about was indeed the same man they'd flown across the world to meet.

As she approached the building Kit felt a tension begin to build inside her. Would Nathan renege on his offer to help Mark build a snowman? she wondered.

Kit pushed open the heavy door and went inside. She stood for several moments simply gazing around. The building was much bigger than she'd first thought and there were enormous stainless steel vats and various pieces of equipment she'd never seen before.

As she pulled off her gloves and tucked them into the pocket of her coat, she noticed an office on her right, its walls comprised mostly of glass. Through the windows Kit saw Nathan, pen in hand, flipping through a pile of papers spread out on top of the desk.

That he was unaware of her arrival was obvious by the fact that he had neither moved nor glanced up on her entrance. His attention was focused on the papers in front of him.

Kit allowed herself the luxury of studying him without being observed. His dark head and handsome features had a noble quality about them and as her gaze drifted from his profile and down to the broad muscular shoulders encased in a dark blue sweater, she felt a quiver of awareness ripple through her.

Almost as if he had sensed her presence Nathan looked up and as their gazes collided Kit was instantly made aware of the power that seemed to emanate from him.

Slowly she walked toward the office door, feeling much as if he were reeling her in on the end of a fishing line.

"What brings you here?" Nathan asked, pushing back his chair and rising to his feet.

Kit moistened lips that were dry and, outwardly at least, tried to appear calm and collected. "Your mother sent me to tell you that it's lunchtime," she said, conscious all the while of his pale eyes studying her.

"Already?" Nathan glanced briefly at the watch on his wrist as he came around the desk. He let his gaze skim over Kit, noting she was wearing Carmen's coat and noticing, too, that it was big for her more delicate frame.

As he came toward her he instantly became aware of the tension within her, a tension she was trying hard to conceal. Intrigued, he came to a halt directly in front of her. Tall as she was, she still had to tilt her head back and as she looked up at him, he had the distinct impression those unusual gray-green eyes of hers were assessing him, and for a fleeting moment he wondered just how he measured up.

Beneath the white knitted ski hat, her hair was pulled away from her face and tied behind her back in a severe style that accentuated those classically high cheekbones that were splashed with red fire, thanks to the winter temperatures outside.

Not for the first time, Nathan found himself trying to imagine what she would look like with her hair flowing free around her face and shoulders or spread out against the backdrop of a white satin pillow.

Annoyance shimmered through him at the direction his thoughts had taken. What was there about this woman that ignited this basic response within him?

She was beautiful, yes. But he'd been made a fool of before by a beautiful woman, a woman who'd manipulated and used him then left him to pick up the pieces. Never again. A wave of pain and anger coursed through him at the memory. Five years was a long time to hold on to such a negative emotion, but somehow it had become a habit, one he'd never bothered to break.

"Tell me," he said, suddenly feeling the need to lash out at someone. "What's the real reason you're here? Did Angela swap stories with you and tell you I was a rich man? Is that why you concocted this story about the boy being mine? Were you hoping to cash in on it?"

As his scathing accusation registered, Nathan saw the initial look of stunned disbelief in her eyes before they darkened to an emerald green.

The urge to slap his face was strong, but Kit held her arms at her sides and stood her ground, determined not to lose her temper. "I neither need nor want any of your money, Mr. Alexander." Kit spat out the words, contempt in every syllable. "Whether you choose to believe it or not, I brought Mark here because I believe he is your son. He needs a father, not a man who's bitter and angry about a past he can't change. While you may have every right to feel the way you do, don't you think it's time to let go, maybe even forgive—" She broke off, sure she was championing a lost cause. "I feel sorry for you . . ."

"Sorry for me?" Nathan's tone was harsh and filled with scorn. "Sorry for me?" he repeated incredulously.

"Yes, I do," Kit responded evenly, ignoring with difficulty the erratic leap of her pulse, due to the fact that he'd taken a step toward her, but she held her ground. "If you persist in wallowing in the past, hiding behind that wall you've built to keep everyone who cares about you away, you're going to end up a very lonely man...just like Ebenezer Scrooge.

"He was a man with no friends, with no one who cared about him, but lucky for him, he came to his senses just in time," she said defiantly. "You're running out of time."

The air between them was rife with tension and Kit felt a tremor race through her as Nathan's eyes bored into hers as if he were trying to see inside her soul.

"Are you telling me you came all the way from England because you care about me, Miss Bellamy?" Nathan's voice reverberated with both anger and sarcasm.

"I care about Mark," Kit replied, wishing he wasn't so near, wishing she hadn't responded to his accusations but had turned and walked out. Now, it was too late.

"If that's true, why are you trying to pawn him off on me?"

Nathan's quick and cruel retort had Kit reeling and before she could stop to think, her hand came up and made resounding contact with his cheek.

Her eyes flew to meet his and for several long seconds she gazed into their startled depths. Appalled at what she had done, she drew a ragged breath and started to turn away, but Nathan's hands came up to stop her. And before she could even begin to struggle, his mouth swooped down to cover hers in a bruising kiss that was solely meant to punish.

The hard-driving pressure of his lips forced hers apart and immediately she felt the hot, sweet invasion of his tongue as it plundered the soft recesses of her mouth.

All at once the tempo changed from hard, fast and furious to slow, soft and seductive and Kit was caught in a dizzying wave of sensation sending her heart hammering erotically against her breast.

A knot of heat began to grow and spread as the taste and the texture of him filled her senses, robbing her of the will to fight, the will to resist. Her hands somehow found their way into his hair and she thrilled at the silky feel of it between her questing fingers.

Even as he crushed her to him he couldn't seem to get close enough. Her softness was as enticing as a feather bed and the heat radiating from her was making his blood sizzle through his veins.

Her mouth tasted of cinnamon and spice and the sweet exotic scent drifting through his senses was arousing an aching need he hadn't felt in a long time.

What on earth was happening to her? Kit felt as if she was spinning out of control, her whole body throbbing with need and tingling with expectancy, waiting... wanting... wanton.

Then all at once it was over and Kit was suddenly standing a few feet away from him, wondering how she got there and trying not only to slow her racing heart but to corral emotions gone hopelessly awry.

The kiss had been a mistake. It meant nothing, nothing at all, she told herself resolutely even as she fought to quell the need he'd so easily aroused.

One kiss, that's all it had been, one incredible, wonderful, heart-wrenching kiss, more devastating than an earthquake, more powerful than a tornado, creating internal chaos.

"I think I'd better go," Kit managed to say as she began to back away.

"Tell my mother I'll be up in a few minutes," Nathan said before he turned and crossed to his desk. He kept his back to her and began to rummage through the papers scattered there, keeping up the pretence of looking for something, until he heard the outer door click shut.

Nathan slumped against the desk and closed his eyes. What had gotten into him? What had possessed him to kiss her that way? He'd been shocked that she'd slapped him, though he acknowledged that she'd had good reason, he'd been inordinately cruel.

He'd deserved her tongue-lashing and he couldn't help admiring her for the way she'd bravely stood up to him. But all he'd been able to think about was the sudden and overwhelming urge to hit back, to retaliate in some way.

He'd wanted to punish her, to vent his own frustration and anger, but the moment his mouth touched hers something had gone desperately wrong.

Nathan closed his eyes, then groaned aloud as the memory of their kiss bombarded him from all sides. He'd never before experienced such an instant awareness, such a powerful jolt of desire. Like two chemicals that shouldn't be mixed in the same test tube, between them they'd created an intense reaction not unlike an explosion.

Spinning the chair around Nathan slowly lowered himself onto the padded seat and waited for his heart rate to return to normal. He wasn't sure how long he sat staring into space, seconds perhaps or maybe even minutes, but when the phone on his desk rang he cursed soundly as he reached for the receiver.

"Where's Nathan? Didn't he come back with you?" Joyce asked as she glanced up from setting a basket of buns on the table.

"He said he'd be here in a minute," Kit replied as she and Mark followed the dogs into the kitchen.

"Hmm . . . how often have I heard that before," Joyce commented almost to herself.

"He won't forget about helping us build a snowman after lunch, will he?" Mark asked, a hint of anxiety in his tone.

"Of course not," Joyce assured him.

"I'm going to pop upstairs for a minute," Kit said, and without waiting for a reply, headed down the hallway. She wanted to be alone, needed to be alone, feeling much as if she'd been tossed around in a windstorm.

Once in her bedroom she closed the door and leaned heavily against it, wondering all the while just how she should act or what she should say to Nathan after what had happened between them.

Her thoughts turned once more to the kiss and she felt her body tremble in reaction. She hugged herself in an attempt to ease the swift yet unmistakable ache of need suddenly clutching at her insides.

Calmly she tried to tell herself that it was utterly ridiculous that she should be attracted to the man who was Mark's father, especially when she wasn't all together sure she even liked him.

He was stubborn and proud—that much was obvious. But his arrogant suggestion that she had ulterior motives for bringing Mark to British Columbia had been cruel and totally unfounded.

She should never have come. She should have ignored Angela's plea to right the wrong she'd done Mark's father, and simply made a life for herself and Mark.

No! The denial came swiftly. Kit knew that she would never have been able to live with the guilt of not trying. She found her thoughts drifting back to her own childhood to those long pain-filled months she'd spent in various foster homes. Those bleak, unhappy days had been erased the moment she'd been told about her grand-mother.

Though Mark's situation wasn't the same as hers had been, Kit still felt strongly that it was her duty to continue her quest to try to reunite Mark with his family.

Their flight back to London was less than two weeks away and Joyce had been kind enough to extend an invitation to stay on until she could talk to Tobias Sheridan in the hope that he might remember her parents.

Having already accepted Joyce's offer, Kit couldn't in all conscience turn around and say she'd changed her mind, that they were leaving. Besides, she owed it to Angela and Mark and, for that matter, to Joyce to keep trying. And perhaps in a strange rather roundabout way she even owed it to Nathan.

Chapter Seven

When Kit returned to the kitchen she was surprised to see Nathan already seated at the table. He stood up as she joined them and for a fraction of a second their eyes met and held, but he gave no sign that anything untoward had passed between them, making her wonder if perhaps the kiss they'd shared had been a figment of her imagination.

"Did Carmen call?" Nathan asked his mother as he sat down again.

"Yes, about fifteen minutes ago," she replied as she began to serve hot vegetable soup from the ceramic soup tureen on the table.

"Where did she spend the night? Not at the clinic, I hope," Nathan added as he offered first Mark and then Kit a bun from the bread basket.

"No. They stayed at Jackson's hotel across the street," Joyce reported, setting a steaming bowl of soup in front of Kit.

"Thank you," Kit murmured.

"They?" Nathan frowned as he set the bread basket down and retrieved a bun for himself.

"Well, Carmen wasn't the only one who couldn't make it home last night," his mother explained.

"Will she be home tonight?" he asked.

"No. She said she's planning on staying in town for another night, at least."

"What's the latest weather report? Are the roads open yet? Are they drivable?" Nathan asked and at his questions Kit threw a startled glance in his direction. Had he changed his mind about the truce? Was he trying to tell her in a subtle way that she should leave?

"The storm warning is over, and I imagine some of the locals are out driving around," Joyce answered. "That four-wheel drive of yours has a good set of snow tires, doesn't it?"

"They're pretty good," Nathan agreed. "But for the drive out to the highway from here you really need a set of chains. I'll put them on after lunch."

"Aren't we going to build a snowman first?" Mark, who had been silent throughout the conversation, was quick to ask.

Kit glanced at Nathan wondering if after their caustic encounter in his office, he might have changed his mind.

"Of course," he assured the boy. "Building a snowman is the first item on my list of things to do this afternoon." At Nathan's words Mark grinned engagingly.

As soon as lunch was over, Mark hopped down from the table and with the dogs at his heels headed to where he'd hung up his outdoor things. Kit followed and helped him with the zipper of his jacket.

"Aren't you coming, too?" Mark asked Kit as he waited for Nathan who was helping his mother clear away the dishes.

"I'll be along shortly, just as soon as the dishes are done," said Kit, all the while thinking that given a choice she would much rather stay indoors, out of Nathan's way altogether.

"Nonsense, my dear," Joyce quickly cut in. "You go with them. I'll have these done in a jiffy."

Kit hesitated and felt her heart shift gears as Nathan joined her by the back door. With Mark, the dogs, herself and now Nathan, the space was somewhat crowded and once again she found his nearness more than a little disconcerting.

"If you're sure," Kit said, deliberately avoiding Nathan's gaze.

"Come on, Kit," Mark urged, anxious to get started.

Suppressing a sigh Kit reached for the coat she'd worn earlier, only to have Nathan take it from her.

"Allow me," he said, and Kit had no option but to accept. His hands brushed her shoulders and at the searing contact she had to steel herself not to react.

His fingers lingered for a moment near her neck as he adjusted the collar, and Kit had to close her eyes as the urge to lean back into his warmth, his strength was almost too much to resist. Only the blast of cold air that swirled around them when Mark opened the door brought her fully alert.

"Thank you," she managed to say as she moved away from him and crouched to locate the winter boots and pull them on, wondering all the while at her body's traitorous response to his nearness. Straightening once more, she fumbled for the gloves she'd tucked into her coat pocket and, forgetting the woolen hat she'd worn earlier, she followed Mark and the dogs outside.

Nathan brought up the rear, closing the door behind them and Mark immediately turned to him.

"Where are we going to build it?" he asked.

Nathan pondered this question for a moment, pulling on his gloves before answering. "Whenever my brother and I built a snowman, we liked to be able to see it from the kitchen window," he said.

"That's a good idea," Mark replied, flashing Kit a smile.

"Now let me see." Nathan moved toward the edge of the patio with Mark at his heels. Bending over he picked up a handful of snow and inspected it closely. Mark quickly copied the action, following Nathan as he crossed the path, coming to a halt in front of some snow-covered bushy evergreens not far from the house.

"What about right here?" Mark suggested gazing up at Nathan for approval.

"Perfect."

Kit felt her eyes sting with tears at the look of pure pleasure that appeared on Mark's upturned face.

The dogs wandered off to explore and as the sun peeked out from behind the clouds Kit almost forgot the chilly temperatures, at least for a little while.

As the afternoon wore on she found herself rethinking her previous stand on whether or not she liked the man who was Mark's father. How could she fail to admire Nathan's enthusiastic, energetic and practical approach to the task of building a snowman?

After showing Mark how to get started by rolling a snowball around gathering more snow, Nathan proceeded to roll one himself, working at it until he had to call both Kit and Mark to help him push it to their allotted site.

"We'll make this part the body," he told them as together they pushed and panted until the huge lump of snow was in place.

"And my part is the head," Mark said. "Is it big enough yet?" he asked.

Nathan glanced at Mark's efforts. "Hey... you're doing a great job," he said and Mark beamed at him in delight. "But I think it needs to be a bit bigger. Come on, I'll give you a hand. Maybe while we do that Kit can smooth off the top to make sure the head won't topple off when we put it on," he added, flashing a fleeting smile in her direction.

Kit could only nod. The smile, warm and friendly, had caught her totally off guard. Was this really the same Nathan Alexander who'd accused her of trying to pawn Mark off on him a few hours ago?

She'd fully expected Nathan to rush through the process of building a snowman, but instead he appeared to be enjoying himself. Either that or he was a damned good actor. But during the past hour and a half Kit hadn't detected any sign that he was bored or restless and impatient to leave.

Turning to see how they were faring she was greeted by two sets of rosy-cheeked, red-nosed, smiling faces. Father and son were heading toward her carrying the snowman's head between them. Nathan was stooping rather awkwardly in an attempt to accommodate Mark's small stature, and watching them Kit felt a warm glow spread through her.

"I'll lift it," Nathan said and Mark immediately released his hold, allowing Nathan to straighten and carefully set the head onto the body.

"Neato!" Mark cried, grinning from ear to ear.

"But it isn't finished yet," Nathan said as he scooped up a handful of snow and used it to cement the head more securely to the body.

"It isn't?" Mark said.

"I think Mr. Frosty here needs eyes, a nose and a mouth. What do you think?" asked Nathan.

"But what do we use?" the boy asked.

"I picked up a couple of small rocks for his eyes, and a broken twig for his mouth," Kit said. "Will they do?"

"But what about a nose?" Mark asked.

"A carrot is what Jon and I always used," Nathan said. "Why don't you go and ask my mother for one."

Almost as if she'd heard his comment Joyce appeared at the back door. "I've been watching from the window. You've done a tremendous job," she told them with a smile. "I was rummaging through the hall closet and found this old hat and scarf. Why don't you put them on the old fellow to keep him warm?"

"Can we have a carrot for his nose?" Mark asked as he ran toward the door.

"Certainly. Wait right there," she told him before disappearing inside.

Kit glanced at Nathan who was carefully shaping Mr. Frosty's head. "Thank you," she said softly and immediately his eyes lifted to meet hers.

"What for?" he asked.

"For being so nice to Mark. He'll remember this for a long time," she said, adding a silent "And so will I." At her words she was surprised to see an emotion she couldn't quite decipher flicker briefly in the pale depths of his eyes.

"I like kids," he said, brushing off her words with a nonchalance he was far from feeling, reluctant to admit even to himself that he'd actually had fun. Though initially he'd been a trifle annoyed at the way he'd been coerced into agreeing to assist, he'd enjoyed himself immensely.

He couldn't remember the last time he'd done anything simply for the fun of it. Perhaps his mother was right. Maybe he did spend too much time overseeing every aspect of the business from picking the grapes to bottling the wine.

But his diligence had paid off, and each year the results proved that his efforts were not in vain, though he had to admit sometimes he often made work for himself.

"Can I put Mr. Frosty's hat and scarf on him?" asked Mark who had appeared at Nathan's side.

"Sure," Nathan replied and bending down he lifted the boy into his arms holding him steady while Mark wrapped the scarf around the snowman's neck and set the hat on his head.

Between the three of them they put the finishing touches to Mr. Frosty and as they stood back to admire their handiwork, Kit noticed that Mark was still holding on tightly to Nathan's hand. Not for the first time she found herself wishing she'd brought her camera downstairs with her. She wondered if Nathan realized that he'd already won himself a place in his young son's heart. The fact that Mark had taken such a shine to Nathan no doubt had to do with the fact that Nathan was the first male adult to have taken any notice of Mark, or spent any quality time with him.

Watching the way Mark interacted with Nathan had also made Kit realize that the youngster needed male companionship in his life, needed a man to look up to, to emulate and what better role model than his real father?

"Mr. Frosty is the bestest looking snowman in the whole world," Mark said, smiling first at Nathan and then at Kit.

"You're right about that," Nathan said with a laugh, the deep warm sound sending a shiver through Kit.

"Can we make another one?" Mark asked, gazing eagerly at Nathan.

"Not today, sport," Nathan said and at his words saw the look of disappointment on the boy's face. "It's going to get dark soon and I have a few things I want to do before then, including putting chains on my truck."

"Can I help?" Mark asked.

"Mark," Kit intervened. "If Mr. Alexander has work to do, why don't I get my camera and take some pictures of you with Mr. Frosty and maybe then Cleo and Piper will have come back from their wanderings and I can take some photos of you and the dogs."

"Okay," said Mark, trying to hide his disappointment as he accepted the compromise.

"Thanks," Nathan said, flashing Kit an appreciative glance. "I'll see you both later," he added before striding away.

"Wait here, Mark," Kit said as she headed for the back door. Once inside Joyce volunteered to go up to Kit's room and bring down her camera bag.

When Kit rejoined Mark outside a few minutes later, her camera in hand, Cleo and Piper had reappeared. For the next fifteen minutes Kit snapped off almost an entire roll of film, before the light began to fade and the afternoon sky began to darken.

"I'm cold," Mark announced and without further ado Kit quickly ushered him inside where Joyce was waiting with mugs of steaming hot chocolate.

They sat at the kitchen table looking outside at Mr. Frosty who seemed to be smiling at them contentedly from the garden. Mark sat quietly, sipping his hot chocolate and Kit could see that he was fighting to stay awake.

"Want to go upstairs and lie down for a while before supper?" Kit asked.

Mark nodded and managed a smile. The crisp country-fresh air and all the activity had sapped his energy and Joyce nodded her approval as Kit lifted Mark off the chair and carried him upstairs.

He was asleep before she reached the top of the stairs. Pushing the bedspread aside she gently laid him down, pulling the cover over him. She bent to kiss his forehead then stroked the soft curve of his cheek. She stood for a long moment staring at this child who had come to mean so much to her.

But watching him interacting with his father, copying Nathan's actions, at times with a look of hero-worship in his eyes, Kit found it difficult to curb some feelings of jealousy and anger.

Jealous because Mark with his incredible capacity to love, had opened his heart to Nathan, unaware of the danger that he might ultimately be rejected. And angry because the love Mark was offering was unconditional and in all probability Nathan would watch them walk away without a second thought.

Kit sighed as she withdrew and made her way downstairs, wondering if she could break down the barriers Nathan had erected.

While Angela had confessed that she'd lied to Nathan, she hadn't explained the reason she'd lied, nor for that matter had she told Kit the circumstances surrounding how her relationship with Nathan Alexander had evolved. All Angela had been concerned about was that Mark should know his father, that Kit should somehow right the wrong she'd done and unite the boy with the only family he had left.

"Kit! I'm here, in the sitting room." Joyce's voice cut through Kit's musings, bringing her to a halt at the bottom of the stairs.

The oak-paneled door on her right was ajar and Kit entered the sitting room to find Joyce sitting in an easy chair in front of a gas fire, knitting.

Crossing the cream-colored carpet Kit glanced around the spacious room admiring the beautiful mahogany baby grand piano sitting in the big bay window that overlooked the driveway.

"Come and sit down," Joyce invited, nodding toward the love seat nearby.

"Thank you," said Kit, all the while thinking how elegant the room was furnished with a collection of rich dark mahogany pieces. At either end of the Queen Anne love seat stood a set of end tables and in front of the fire a matching coffee table, its surface gleaming in the flickering gaslight telling of the love and care it obviously received.

The love seat itself was a dusky rose pink and as Kit sat down she felt at home in the warm ambience of the room.

"He's asleep?" Joyce asked, glancing up from the sweater she was knitting.

"Out like a light," Kit replied with a smile as she sat down opposite Joyce.

"Watching you out there today reminded me of the times my boys played in the snow with their father," Joyce said with more than a hint of nostalgia in her voice. "You all appeared to be having a good time...even Nathan." She sent a twinkling glance toward Kit.

"I know Mark enjoyed himself," Kit said. "Nathan was really great with him."

"Nathan's always had a soft spot for kids. He'd make a wonderful father. I just wish—" Joyce broke off, lowering her head for a moment before continuing. "I'm sorry, my dear, I don't mean to bore you with an old woman's dreams," she went on with a watery smile.

"You could never be boring," Kit said sincerely, thinking perhaps if Joyce were to confide in her, she might gain some insight into exactly the kind of man Nathan was.

Joyce stopped knitting and lowered the needles onto her lap staring thoughtfully into space for several long moments. "I thought that by now I'd be a grandmother, several times over," Joyce began slowly. "But I suppose it wasn't meant to be." She sighed. "Jon and Carmen had only been married a year when he was killed. Nathan was married, too, but only for a brief time. That was about five years ago." She fell silent once more and Kit said nothing, waiting for her to continue.

"That marriage was a mistake. A huge mistake." Joyce continued, shaking her head at the memory.

"I'm sorry," Kit said, sympathy echoing in her voice.

"As far as I could see, it was doomed from the start," said Joyce, a faint censure in her voice now.

"That's too bad." Kit wished she didn't feel as if she were spying.

"Well, for one thing it all came about so suddenly and unexpectedly," Joyce said, obviously warming up to the topic. "He'd gone to California to attend a symposium on wine making and to tour several of the small estate wineries in both the Napa and Sonoma Valleys. When he returned two weeks later he brought home a bride.

"Her name was Angela. She was a model, from England. A very pretty girl, though personally I found her a bit brittle," Joyce said almost to herself. "They met at a cocktail party and according to Angela that was it…but…" Her voice trailed off and she sat staring into the fire for a long moment.

"But you had reservations," Kit said and at her words Joyce turned to look at her.

"Yes, I did," she said, her expression one of relief that someone understood. "Oh, at first everything appeared rosy. But I had the feeling that Angela hadn't expected the winery to be so isolated." Joyce drew a breath and continued. "They'd only been home a few days when I heard them arguing. It was mid-August, when the grapes are being harvested, that's the busiest time of the year around here. Everyone was working around the clock, especially Nathan. Jon was traveling through Europe at the time, and even though Nathan had hired extra workers he still liked to oversee everything himself.

"I spent most of my time here in the house with Angela and I watched her grow increasingly bored and annoyed at Nathan's lack of attention. She talked on the phone every day to someone in California and I would have had to be blind not to see that things were not going well between her and Nathan."

"I guess they were both under a lot of pressure," Kit said, trying to be fair, yet knowing all the while that Angela had been a city girl through and through.

"Yes, that's true," Joyce acknowledged. "But a marriage, or any relationship for that matter only survives if the two people involved are willing to meet each other halfway, to take the good times with the bad." Joyce stopped and shook her head. "Listen to me, I sound like an advice columnist." She laughed but there was little humor in her voice.

"That sounded to me like good advice," Kit replied.

"Well, I didn't interfere, I couldn't," she said. "And lo and behold a month and a half later Angela walked out, back to California, no doubt. Nathan didn't go after her but I know he's still angry and bitter. That was five years ago. I wish he'd just let go of the past. He made a mistake, that's all. He's human like the rest of us and mistakes are all part of life."

"Sometimes it's harder to forgive yourself than it is to forgive someone else," Kit said soothingly.

Joyce nodded and managed a smile. "I'm sorry, I can't think what came over me, rambling on this way. You should have stopped me," she remarked as she picked up the wool from her lap and began knitting once more.

Kit said nothing, sensing that while Joyce might be a little embarrassed at having revealed quite so much about her son, she'd obviously needed to talk to release some of her own pent up feelings and frustrations.

They sat in silence for a long moment, the only sound the faint clicking of knitting needles as Joyce worked on the sweater.

"It does my heart good to have a child around the place," Joyce said, breaking the silence. "Ah, well, perhaps I'll be a grandmother, yet," she added on a wistful note.

Pain stabbed at Kit's heart at the sorrow and longing she could hear in Joyce's voice, and it was all she could do not to blurt out the truth.

"Surely there's still plenty of time," Kit said, wanting to somehow offer the older woman hope.

"Plenty of time for what?" At the sound of Nathan's deep resonant voice Kit felt her heart jump into her throat. How long had he been listening? How much had he heard?

Chapter Eight

"Plenty of time for grandchildren," Joyce explained calmly, continuing to knit.

Kit knew by the way the hairs stood up at the back of her neck that Nathan was staring at her, and she lifted her gaze to meet his, seeing instantly the question shimmering in the depths of his eyes.

She responded with a quick shake of her head, all the while aware of the tension crackling between them, a tension that intensified a hundredfold the moment he sat down next to her on the love seat.

"Having a cosy little chat about me, were you?" Nathan asked, the edge to his voice making his mother look up from her knitting.

"Yes, we were," his mother replied, obviously not in the least embarrassed by Nathan's displeasure.

"I hope you didn't bore Kit too much," he said as he relaxed against the seat, placing his arm along its back.

"Don't be rude," his mother scolded. "I was telling Kit how much I was enjoying having young Mark around and that I wished I had some grandchildren of my own to spoil, that's all," she told him matter-of-factly and without apology.

"I see," he said, turning toward Kit, an action that brought his knee against hers. A tremor raced through her and it was all she could do not to jerk away from the contact.

With a nonchalance she was far from feeling, Kit stood up. "I'd better check on Mark," she said, making her way around the love seat and away from Nathan.

"Dinner should be ready in about half an hour," Joyce said.

"Is there anything I can do in the meantime?" Kit asked, suddenly feeling guilty that she hadn't made the offer sooner.

"Thank you, my dear, but everything is under control." Joyce assured her.

With a nod Kit turned and made her way from the sitting room wondering if Nathan would ask his mother to elaborate more on precisely what they'd been talking about.

That Joyce Alexander was quite capable of holding her own as far as her son was concerned was apparent. Kit smiled to herself, liking the woman's straightforward, no-nonsense approach to life more and more.

Mark almost collided with Kit as he came hurrying out of the bathroom.

"Hey...what's all the hurry?" Kit asked as she caught him and lifted him into her arms.

"I just wanted to make sure Mr. Frosty was still there," Mark said.

"Oh, he is," Kit laughingly assured him. "I bet you can see him from my bedroom window," she added and Mark wriggled out of her arms to run ahead of her into her room.

"You're right, I can see him." Mark grinned at Kit from the window.

"Why don't you draw a picture of him?" Kit suggested, thinking it might be wise to keep him occupied until it was time to go downstairs for dinner.

"Okay." Mark ran into the next room to find his knapsack. "I'm going to draw a picture of you and me and Mr. Alexander building the snowman," Mark said when he returned carrying his box of crayons and looseleaf binder.

While Mark lay on his stomach on the floor and busied himself drawing, Kit sat down at the dressing table and began to unbraid her hair, an action she found ultimately soothing.

Her long silky tresses, with just a hint of a curl, almost reached her waist and though there had been times when she'd considered having it cut, or trying a new sophisticated style, she'd never been able to go through with it.

One of the strongest memories she had of her childhood was the prebedtime ritual of sitting on her mother's lap while she brushed and braided her long hair. It was a memory Kit found comforting, a memory that evoked feelings of warmth and love.

"How do you like my picture?" Mark asked, hopping to his feet a few minutes later holding out a page for her to inspect.

"That's terrific, Mark," Kit enthused, smiling at him.

"I'm going to take it downstairs with me," he said as he bent to retrieve the crayons still on the floor.

"Good idea," Kit said as she glanced at her watch. "Look at the time. We'd better get moving. We don't want to be late for dinner." She quickly tied her hair with a silk scarf at her nape.

Mark's picture was duly admired by both Joyce and Nathan and earned pride of place on the refrigerator, but throughout the meal Kit sensed a tension in the air and wondered at its cause.

"I insist on doing the dishes tonight," Kit said as soon as the meal was over.

"Thank you, my dear. That would be nice. I noticed earlier that one of my favorite Christmas movies, *It's a Wonderful Life* is on television tonight. It starts in a few minutes."

"Can I watch it, too?" Mark asked, his face lighting up at the mention of television.

"Of course you may watch it with me," Joyce answered. "As long as it's all right with Kit." She glanced at Kit.

"That's one of my favorites, too," Kit replied as she began to gather the dishes, easily recalling the delightful story of George Bailey and Clarence the angel who came down to earth to help him.

Cleo and Piper, who'd been lying quietly on the floor, got to their feet as Nathan pushed back his chair. "I'll give you a hand with the dishes just as soon as I've fed the dogs," he said to Kit and she felt her heart kick against her rib cage in alarm.

"Can I help?" Mark asked, the movie forgotten for the moment.

"I'll go and turn on the television in the sitting room," Joyce said. "When you've finished helping Nathan feed the dogs you can join me there."

Kit filled the sink with hot water and proceeded to clear the remaining dishes from the table while Mark helped Nathan. Moments later Mark reappeared and with a grin and a wave he ran through the kitchen on his way to the sitting room and the television.

Hearing the sound of the back door closing, Kit drew a steadying breath as she waited for Nathan to rejoin her.

"If you have something more important to do, I can easily manage these," she told him when he appeared.

"It'll get done faster when there's two of us," he said, dismissing her subtle hint. Crossing to stand beside her, he picked up a dish towel.

Kit tried with difficulty to ignore the man only a few inches away. She focused her attention on the task in hand but found it increasingly disturbing when their bodies constantly touched or brushed lightly against each other.

She felt her stomach muscles tighten as an unfamiliar ache slowly began to spread through her. What was it about this man that affected her so profoundly? Every nerve, every cell tingled with awareness, a reaction that was fast eroding the slippery hold she had on her composure.

They worked silently and efficiently for ten minutes until the last piece of cutlery was dried and put away, and Kit couldn't help thinking they could easily be mistaken for a married couple who washed the dishes together every night.

This thought, however, only served to escalate the tension simmering inside her and as she let the water drain away she prayed that Nathan was unaware of the turmoil going on inside her.

"Tell me. What exactly were you and my mother talking about earlier?" he asked, surprising her with the question.

Stalling for time, Kit reached for the towel hanging over the oven door and began to dry her hands. "Didn't Joyce tell you?" she asked casually, keeping her tone even as she turned to face him.

"No," Nathan replied. "She just said that watching us build a snowman with Mark brought back memories of my father doing the same with my brother and me."

Kit silently digested this, deciding that if his mother hadn't told him she'd spoken rather openly of Nathan's disastrous marriage to Angela, Kit wasn't about to bring up the subject, either. "Actually that was all we did talk about," Kit responded evenly.

"Liar," Nathan said. He grabbed the other end of her towel and gave it a sharp tug, bringing a startled Kit stumbling against him.

His arms instantly went around her making it impossible to escape, and she had to tilt her head back in order to see his face, an action that sent the silk scarf tied loosely around her hair sliding to the floor.

As her hair was freed from the confines of the knot it spread-eagled across her back and over his hands.

Nathan stiffened in stunned surprise as a silky waterfall cascaded over his wrists and hands. Enthralled, he gently clutched a handful of her hair in each hand, finding its texture as seductive and erotic as a lover's touch.

He felt his heart accelerate, tripping over itself in eager anticipation as the scent of lemon and jasmine assaulted his senses, awakening a need that caught him totally off guard.

He felt trapped in time, afraid to move forward, unwilling to step back. He'd known desire before, felt it scramble through his system to stir his blood and invade his senses . . . but not like this . . . never like this, propel-

ling him with devastating swiftness and leaving him tee-
tering on the edge of reason.

He threaded his fingers through the silky mass of her
hair, cupping the back of her head, holding her exactly
where he wanted her. His lips found the pulse at the side
of her forehead and as he felt the fluttering movement
against his mouth, he reveled in the knowledge that her
pulse was beating almost as fast as his.

Slowly, seductively, he began to trace a path across the
planes of her cheek, drinking in the dark, dusky fra-
grance of her delicate skin, only stopping when he reached
his ultimate destination, her mouth.

Kit felt as if her whole body was being rocked by a small
earthquake. From the moment she'd found herself in his
arms all coherent thought had left her. Beneath her
splayed fingers she could feel the frantic drumming of his
heart and she waited with heady anticipation until she felt
his breath mingle with hers as his mouth hovered only
inches away.

She whispered his name but it was lost in a kiss that
shuddered through her like an aftershock, leaving in its
wake a cavalcade of sensations that sent her reeling.

So this was desire, she thought as she instinctively and
willingly responded to the wild mastery of his mouth, unable to deny herself what she hadn't known she'd been
missing, until now.

A yearning sharp and insistent tugged at her insides,
spreading like wildfire through her, igniting a hunger
she'd never known before, a hunger she knew only he
could appease.

All at once it was over and he was holding her at arm's
length. "This is insane!" Nathan said, his voice husky
and more than a little breathless. "What are you? Some

kind of witch?'' he asked, retreating another step and running a trembling hand through his hair.

The haze of desire swirling around Kit dissipated in an instant when she found herself no longer in the warm circle of his arms.

In the chilly aftermath Kit forced herself to take a steadying breath, fighting to restore order to emotions gone dangerously awry. It took every ounce of strength to meet his gaze, and she did, unflinchingly, refusing to shoulder the blame for the passion that had erupted between them.

He'd kissed her! she thought indignantly and for a fleeting moment at least, he had the good grace to look slightly abashed.

Nathan swore under his breath, totally unnerved by the way he'd lost control. He hadn't intended to kiss her, but somehow the moment he'd touched her, he hadn't been able to deny himself the sweet ecstasy he knew he would taste on her lips.

There was an innate innocence, a heart-wrenching honesty in her response that threatened to erode the wall he'd so painstakingly built around his heart.

He'd vowed never again to let a woman get close enough to trample his emotions and walk all over his heart, but a moment ago he'd been floundering in a pool of sensation and in grave danger of forgetting the painful lessons he'd learned.

"Kit, are you finished?'' Mark, who'd come running into the kitchen, came to an abrupt halt. His glance shifted from one adult to the other, and the puzzled expression on his face told her that he sensed the tension shimmering in the air.

"Yes, I believe we're quite finished,'' Kit said, the barest hint of sarcasm creeping into her voice.

"The movie is going to start in a few minutes. There was a cartoon special on first. Want to watch the show with us?" He directed the question at both of them.

"That sounds lovely," Kit said easily, giving Mark a smile.

"Thanks, Mark, but I'm not one for watching television." Nathan retreated toward the back door.

"Let's go," Kit said, distracting the boy, fearful that he might try to persuade Nathan to change his mind. "We don't want to miss the beginning."

The opening credits for the show were in fact already rolling across the screen, and Kit was grateful that she didn't have to make conversation with Joyce, who flashed her a smile before returning her attention to the set.

Kit found it difficult to keep her attention focused on the action on the screen, her thoughts continually returning to those moments in the kitchen when Nathan had kissed her. She tried to tell herself that she didn't even like the man, that she wasn't in the least attracted to him, but she knew in a corner of her heart that she was lying to herself.

As the movie drew to its highly emotional conclusion, Kit couldn't stop the tears from overflowing, but she wasn't altogether sure if her tears were tears of joy for George and Mary Bailey or tears of self-pity.

Chapter Nine

Kit spent the night tossing and turning as images of Nathan invaded her dreams. She lay awake in the early hours of the morning listening to the wind whistling through the trees outside. Resolutely she reminded herself that Mark's happiness and emotional well-being were her first priority and she should not allow herself to be distracted by whatever chemistry was happening between her and Nathan.

Though Nathan's initial reaction to their arrival had been understandable, she had good reason to hope that he might not be averse to accepting the child as his. And as for Mark, Kit was sure he would be thrilled to discover that the man he admired and looked up to was in actual fact his real father.

Still it was much too soon to be anticipating a happy ending for Mark. Angela had hurt Nathan very badly and Kit knew that until he let go of that past hurt, until he could forgive Angela and himself for the mistakes they'd made, she still had an uphill fight.

Kit glanced at the clock on the night table. It was almost seven-thirty and she knew Mark would be awake soon. She pushed the bedcovers aside and crossed to the window to open the draperies, noting as she did that it had snowed during the night.

The snowman's hat was covered with a fresh layer of white and Kit smiled for a moment, recalling the fun they'd all had building Mr. Frosty.

Just as she was about to withdraw, Nathan's tall, imposing figure suddenly came into view. Dressed in hip-hugging blue jeans and a bulky ski jacket, he was carrying a snow shovel in his gloved hands.

Kit's heart skipped a beat as she let her gaze slide over his muscular frame. He really was quite devastatingly handsome, she thought as she stood watching him begin to clear the path to the winery. With easy strokes he scooped the snow onto the shovel and tossed it aside.

She continued to watch him work swiftly and efficiently for several minutes, until she heard a sound from the adjoining room warning her that Mark had awakened.

Half an hour later, dressed in a pair of blue jeans and a hand-knit sweater, Kit followed Mark down the stairs. In the kitchen Joyce told them that Nathan had already eaten breakfast and would be out until after lunch.

While Mark's disappointment at being left behind was obvious, Kit managed to hide hers. They spent the morning playing games and watching television and as lunchtime came and went Kit found she missed Nathan almost as much as Mark.

The sound of the front door opening and dogs barking had Mark out of the chair, where he'd been curled up watching a children's program, and running from the living room. It was as he raced across the tiled foyer that he slipped on some wet snow brought in by the dogs, and collided with Nathan, sending them both sprawling on the floor.

Mark instantly hopped to his feet, none the worse for the mishap. But as Kit hurried to where Nathan was shifting to a sitting position, she saw that his lips were drawn in a line of pain.

"Are you all right?" Kit asked, concern in her voice.

"No, I'm not all right," Nathan responded flatly, grimacing as he put pressure on his right foot.

"I...I'm sorry...I didn't mean to..." Mark said, tears already gathering in his eyes as he stood beside Nathan, an anxious expression on his small face.

"I heard a crash. What happened?" Joyce appeared from the kitchen.

"It was an accident," Nathan was quick to respond. "I ran into Mark." He flashed a brief but reassuring smile at the boy.

"Where does it hurt?" Kit asked, crouching in front of him.

Nathan shifted and tried to stand up. "Ah...!" He moaned before clamping his jaw shut.

"Cleo! Piper! Stay in the kitchen you two," Joyce ordered as the dogs appeared. "It's not broken, is it?" At this question Kit noticed Mark's lower lip begin to quiver and a tear spilled over to trace a path down his cheek.

"No, I don't think so," Nathan said. "Hey, sport, don't cry." His tone was gentle. "I don't break easily. We men are made of strong stuff, right?" he added, giving Mark an encouraging look.

Mark nodded and sniffed, wiping his eyes with the sleeve of his shirt, even managing a faint but fleeting smile.

"Let's take a look," said Kit and with great care removed Nathan's boot. As she carefully eased off his sock she noticed immediately that the area atop his instep was already starting to swell. She threw a glance at Nathan and as their eyes met there flashed between them a silent communication, an understanding that Mark not be made to feel any worse than he already did.

"Ice. That's what you need," Kit said.

"I'll get some from the fridge," Joyce responded immediately retreating into the kitchen.

"Mark? Go with my mother and help her with the ice, would you?" Nathan instructed.

Mark nodded and quickly followed Joyce.

"I don't think it's broken," said Kit cautiously, as soon as Mark was out of earshot. "But there are so many bones in one's foot it might be wise to have it X-rayed."

"Unfortunately I agree," Nathan said, grimacing once more as he tried to move. "Help me up onto that chair." Kit quickly stood to assist him.

With his weight on his left foot Nathan put his arm around Kit and stood. Bracing herself to act as a crutch, Kit tried to ignore the tingling heat his touch evoked. It was almost like being in his arms, she thought as he carefully maneuvered himself onto the nearby chair.

"Here's the ice," Mark said as he reappeared carrying a bag of ice wrapped in a towel.

"Thanks, Mark," Kit said, taking the towel from him.

"Will your foot really be all right?" Mark asked as he hovered on the sidelines.

"Absolutely," Nathan assured him. "But Kit thinks it might be wise to get it X-rayed, just to make sure nothing's broken."

"Will that hurt?" Mark asked, anxiety edging his voice as he glanced at Kit.

"X rays don't hurt," she replied. "Remember when you fell off the swing at the park and I took you to the hospital? You had an X ray then."

Mark nodded, his eyes still on Nathan.

"But how will you manage to drive?" Joyce asked as she joined them.

"No problem. I'll drive," Kit said.

With Joyce's and Mark's assistance Nathan was soon seated in the passenger seat of his four-wheel-drive van, his right foot carefully wrapped in a blanket, a bag of ice nestled gently on top of the swelling.

Kit had driven the van from the garage to the house without event, grateful for the chains Nathan had put on the tires, which gave added traction in the snow. She put the van into gear once more and made her way along the driveway, managing a smile and wave at Joyce and Mark who were standing at the front door.

The journey out to the highway proved to be easier than she'd anticipated and Nathan sat quietly throughout, offering a few words of encouragement as she negotiated several of the winding curves.

Once on the main highway the going was much easier and twenty-five minutes later Kit, following Nathan's directions, pulled up outside the Medical Clinic located on Meadowvale's main street.

"Wait here, I'll see if I can get a wheelchair for you," Kit said as she hopped onto the snow-covered street.

Kit hurried into the building and at her entrance several people turned to look at her. A handsome man wearing a doctor's white coat atop navy slacks and a blue shirt came toward her.

"Hello!" He greeted Kit with a friendly smile. "Is everything all right?" he asked.

"I need a wheelchair...my friend is injured," Kit said.

"Where is your friend?" the doctor asked.

"Outside in the van," said Kit. "He fell and hurt his foot," she explained.

"I'm Dr. McGregor," he said. "There's a wheelchair right here." He moved to an alcove Kit hadn't noticed to retrieve the chair. "Lead the way."

Kit turned and headed back through the automatic doors, with the doctor pushing the wheelchair, close behind. Nathan stood on the snowy sidewalk, leaning on the van door for support, a grim look on his face.

"Nathan! What happened to you?" the doctor asked.

"Hello, Bruce," Nathan responded. "I slipped and fell and somehow twisted my foot on the way down," he explained. "What are you doing in Meadowvale? This isn't one of your usual days at the clinic, is it?"

"No... Here, take it easy. Turn around...that's right." Dr. McGregor steadied the wheelchair as Nathan lowered himself into it.

Kit retrieved her purse from the floor of the passenger side, then closed the door. "Will it be all right to leave the van here?" she asked.

"No problem," the doctor assured her as he began to push the wheelchair through the doorway.

"Bruce, this is Kit Bellamy," said Nathan over his shoulder.

"Hello, Kit," Bruce said. "If you'd like to wait right here, I'll wheel him down to the X-ray lab. It won't take long."

Kit nodded and watched for a moment until the doctor pushed Nathan's wheelchair into an elevator. Glancing around she noticed a small reception area with several chairs and a table with magazines, and crossed to sit and wait.

Twenty minutes later Kit glanced toward the elevators in time to see Dr. McGregor emerge, alone. Rising to her feet she went to meet him.

"No broken bones. Just a sprained ankle," said the doctor as he drew near. "If you'd like to come this way, I'll take you to him."

Kit nodded, relieved to hear the news.

"Applying ice was the best course of action," she heard the doctor say as he ushered her through a set of doors into what appeared to be a fairly large, emergency room. A row of beds with curtains around them, took up most of the area.

Two of the beds were occupied by young children, their parents standing nearby, offering comfort. Kit scanned the room, easily locating Nathan stretched out on one of the beds, smiling at a tall, very attractive, dark-haired woman.

Kit felt a sharp stab of pain, somewhere near the region of her heart, at the sight of Nathan talking so animatedly to the woman at his bedside. Her footsteps slowed as the urge to turn and leave was strong. But, aware of the doctor directly behind her, she forced herself to move toward the bed.

Nathan glanced at Kit as she approached and his smile widened sending her heart into a tailspin.

"You must be Kit," said the smartly dressed woman as she came around the bed to greet her.

"Yes, I am," Kit managed to say, reluctantly dragging her eyes from Nathan's.

"I'm Carmen, Nathan's sister-in-law," the woman said extending her hand.

"Oh . . . yes," Kit responded, remembering now that Joyce had mentioned that Carmen worked at the clinic. "Nice to meet you." Kit shook the offered hand.

"Nathan's just been telling me about your arrival at the house. You're on holiday from England, with your little boy, I hear."

Kit flashed a brief glance at Nathan before answering. "Yes. We're just touring around," Kit replied, sure by Carmen's friendly manner that Nathan hadn't told his sister-in-law the real reason for Kit's visit. "The snowstorm caught us unawares. But thankfully Mrs. Alexander was kind enough to extend us her hospitality."

"That was quite a storm," Bruce said, moving to stand next to Carmen, smiling down at her. "I decided the roads were too treacherous to attempt to drive home, and I told Carmen I didn't think she should drive, either. We ended up spending the night at the hotel across the street."

At the implication in Bruce's words a blush swept over Carmen's cheeks, and Kit noticed the look that passed between the doctor and Nathan's sister-in-law, making her wonder if there was a romance in the offing. Certainly the signs were all there, she thought.

"Bruce was kind enough to buy me dinner," Carmen explained and the sparkle in her brown eyes told a story all its own. Kit smiled to herself.

"We had no problem driving in," Nathan said rather abruptly. "You'll be able to get home tonight, Carmen. You too, Doctor."

Puzzled by Nathan's disapproving tone Kit turned to look at the man on the bed, seeing the frown on his features.

"Ah, yes, I suppose you're right," Carmen said, though there was no mistaking the disappointment in her tone. "I've got a few things to do before I leave, so I'd better get back to work. Nice to meet you, Kit. I'll see you both at home, later," she added before turning and walking away.

"Now tell me, Bruce, when can I get out of here?" Nathan asked once Carmen had left.

"I'll have a nurse put a light supportive bandage on your ankle, then you can be on your way," Bruce said. "Pick up a pair of crutches before you go, and just stay off it as much as possible. You should be able to put some pressure on it by the weekend."

By the time Nathan and Kit set out on the homeward journey it was growing dark. The colorful Christmas lights strung at intervals along the main street added a festive air to the town and the thick blanket of snow on the ground afforded a good deal of light as they drove out of Meadowvale.

"How long has your sister-in-law worked at the clinic?" Kit asked, breaking the silence.

"Over a year now," Nathan replied.

"Where does Dr. McGregor usually work?" Kit asked.

"At the hospital in Peachville. He drives over to the clinic every Monday," Nathan explained.

Kit could tell by the short and rather abrupt answers Nathan was supplying that he wasn't in the mood to talk. She wondered whether he was in pain, or simply frustrated that the journey had for all intents and purposes been a waste of time.

"What did you think of the good doctor?" Nathan asked, breaking a silence that had lasted more than five minutes, and telling Kit clearly that he'd been quietly speculating on the relationship between his sister-in-law and Dr. McGregor.

"He seemed very nice. Why?" Kit asked, glancing at him briefly before turning her attention to the road ahead.

"There's something going on between those two," Nathan mumbled and Kit almost laughed aloud at his disgruntled tone.

"How long has Carmen been a widow?" Kit asked, though she already knew the answer.

"Two years," came the reply. "It's just that—" Nathan broke off, surprised and annoyed to suddenly find himself on the verge of discussing with this woman who was a stranger, his feelings regarding his sister-in-law's budding relationship with his friend Bruce McGregor.

"It's just that what?" she asked him, her tone reasonable, her voice faintly persuasive.

"I don't know." He blurted out the answer almost angrily, unsure now why the thought of Carmen and Bruce finding happiness together should bother him. But it did. "I suppose I feel a certain responsibility for her because she was married to my brother."

"How did he die?" Kit's voice was soft and low and strangely soothing and Nathan suddenly found himself relating the story of how he'd left Jon in charge of the winery and driven to Vancouver for the weekend to attend one of the city's most prestigious antique shows.

It was a trip he made each and every November in order to browse the numerous stalls in search of antique corkscrews or other wine memorabilia to add to his collection.

He'd been sitting in his hotel room inspecting and admiring the two corkscrews he'd bought that afternoon after much dickering with one of the dealers at the show, when this mother called.

He barely remembered the drive home and he'd never quite been able to forgive himself for not being there for his mother, or for Carmen; that he'd been off enjoying himself while his brother lay dying after a drunk driver crossed the median and plowed headlong into Jon's car.

Kit heard the guilt in Nathan's voice and her heart went out to him. That he cared for and felt protective toward his sister-in-law was apparent. She'd seen the friendly rapport that existed between them as well as the affection, and Kit sensed that Nathan had played an important part in helping Carmen deal with her husband's death.

But Kit had also seen the way Bruce had looked at Carmen, she'd seen the spark of attraction shimmering between them, and wondered if Nathan, who she felt sure had witnessed it, too, was finding it difficult to face the fact that Carmen might no longer need him, that she was ready to move on with her life.

"You may not want to hear this," Kit said, her words drawing a curious glance from the man seated beside her.

"That's never stopped you before," Nathan said gruffly.

"I'd say Carmen has worked through her grief, she's ready to move on with her life, put the past behind her," she began.

"Don't stop now," Nathan said.

"If they are falling in love..." She hesitated for a moment, glancing at Nathan in order to gauge his reaction to this statement, but all she saw was a shadowed profile in the dim interior of the van, a profile that told her nothing at all.

Kit remained silent while she negotiated the final curve, which brought the house into view. "Well . . ." she continued into the darkness. "Falling in love doesn't happen by order or design, it just happens, and if that's what's happening between Carmen and Bruce, I'm afraid there's nothing you can do about it," she concluded as she brought the van to a halt behind her rented car.

Whatever response Nathan might have offered was lost as the light from the front door as it opened spilled over them. Kit quickly jumped down from the driver's seat and came around to give Nathan a hand with the crutches.

In the doorway Joyce and Mark stood waiting expectantly, and Kit could hear the dogs barking from somewhere in the house. Loath to offer help that she felt sure would be rejected, Kit simply stayed behind Nathan as he struggled with the crutches, finally reaching the house without incident.

"There you are!" said his mother with more than a hint of relief in her voice.

"Is your foot broke?" Mark asked, his anxious expression bringing a lump to Kit's throat.

"No, it's just bruised. I'll be as good as new in a couple of days," Nathan added lightly. "We're starving, what's for supper?"

"I shut the dogs in the laundry room when I saw the van's lights," said his mother. "And unless you want them to knock you over again, you'd better hobble into the sitting room and I'll bring you your dinner on a tray."

"Hey, Mark. Open up that door for me, will you?" Nathan said, and eager to assist in any way, Mark ran on ahead of his father.

Kit followed Joyce into the kitchen.

"You look tired, my dear. How were the roads?" Joyce asked.

"Not too bad, actually," Kit replied. "I met your daughter-in-law, Carmen, at the clinic," she added.

"Did she say if she'd be home tonight?" Joyce asked.

"Yes, I'm sure she will," Kit replied. "I hope Mark wasn't too much trouble," she said, wondering how they'd spent the afternoon.

"No trouble at all," came the prompt reply. "We had a wonderful time. We played cards, took the dogs for a short walk and then Mark sat at the table and drew me a picture while I made supper," she told Kit. "I think I hear a car. That's probably Carmen, now."

Several minutes later the back door opened and Carmen entered. "Hello, Kit. Hi, Joyce. I'm back," she said as she pulled off her gloves and removed her full-length woolen overcoat. "Something smells good," she commented as she crossed to give Joyce a warm hug. "How are you?" she asked.

"Fine, just fine," Joyce said.

"Where's Nathan?" Carmen asked. "Don't tell me you persuaded him to rest his foot in bed?"

"That'll be the day," Joyce responded with a laugh. "No, he's in the sitting room with Mark."

"Mark? Oh, right, Mark is your son," said Carmen turning to Kit.

"Not exactly," Kit replied. "I'm his guardian. Mark was my best friend Ang—" she broke off "—my best friend's son," Kit amended quickly, relieved to note that Joyce was giving her attention to something on the stove.

"Oh, I see," said Carmen at the same moment that Mark came barreling into the kitchen.

"We heard a car...oh...hello!" He stopped and smiled up at Carmen.

"Hello, yourself. I'm Carmen," she said and Kit saw the puzzled look that creased her pretty features as she gazed at the boy.

"I'm Mark," he told her.

"Pleased to meet you, Mark," Carmen replied, throwing a frowning glance at Kit.

"Do you live here, too?" Mark asked.

"Yes, I do," she answered.

"Supper's almost ready." Joyce jumped in, effectively distracting their attention.

"Do I have time to run upstairs and change?" Carmen asked.

"Of course, my dear," Joyce responded. "Kit, perhaps you'd like a chance to freshen up, too?"

"Yes, thank you, I would," Kit said.

"I'll put Mark's and Nathan's dinner on a tray. They can eat in the sitting room in front of the television," said Joyce. "That way, we womenfolk can have a friendly chat right here," she proposed with a smile.

"Good idea," said Carmen before making her way from the kitchen.

As Kit followed, she wondered if the reason for Carmen's puzzled expression a few moments ago was the fact that she had noticed how much Mark resembled Nathan.

"Did you say you were Mark's guardian?" Carmen asked as they crossed the tiled foyer and began to climb the stairs.

"That's right," Kit said.

"Was his mother's name Angela, by any chance?"

Kit felt her mouth drop open in astonishment at the question. "How did you...?" she began to ask then abruptly broke off, realizing that she'd just answered the question.

"You started to say Angela," Carmen replied. "That's what got me thinking. I remember Jon saying that Nathan had been married briefly to an English model called Angela," she explained. "I never met her, but that, plus the fact Mark looks so much like Nathan...well, I just put two and two together. Does Joyce know?"

Kit shook her head.

"What about Nathan?" Carmen asked.

"Yes, I told him Mark is his son," Kit answered. "But he doesn't believe me."

"Then he's a blind fool," Carmen announced, making Kit smile. "Is that why you came here?" she asked.

"Yes," Kit responded, relieved to have at least that truth out in the open. "I thought if I brought Mark and his father together, I might make Nathan see..." She stopped thinking for the first time that her plan had really been no plan at all.

"What about Angela?" Carmen asked.

"She died six months ago," Kit replied.

"I'm sorry..." Carmen responded. "Why didn't she tell Nathan she was pregnant?"

"Nathan did know," Kit replied. "But Angela told him the baby wasn't his."

"And he believed her?"

Kit nodded. "Before she died Angela told me she'd lied to him about everything and she begged me to try to unite Mark with his father."

"That's quite an undertaking. How long are you staying? When do you go back to England?" Carmen asked.

"A few days before Christmas," Kit answered.

"Then what you need is a miracle."

Chapter Ten

The remainder of the week passed quickly. Kit found that having Carmen as a friend and ally somehow helped to keep up her own spirits.

At first Nathan proved to be a rather uncooperative patient, no doubt due to the fact that the injury restricted his movements and it took a little time to master the crutches. Getting downstairs each morning became something of challenge.

Strangely it was Mark, with his sense of fun and outgoing personality, who managed to cajole Nathan out of his initial ill temper. And it was Mark who happily took on the job of keeping Nathan occupied throughout the day, by playing card games with him, running errands for him and generally keeping him company. In return Nathan entrusted Mark with the care and feeding of the dogs, a task he undertook with great pride.

It was with mixed emotions that Kit watched the relationship between Mark and his father slowly take root.

Often as Kit helped Joyce in the kitchen, they would hear the sound of Nathan's deep laugh echoing through the house, and seeing the smile that always lit up Joyce's face, Kit was sorely tempted to divulge the truth about Mark.

That Nathan would indeed make a wonderful father was easy to see, but while both Nathan and Mark appeared to be enjoying their developing relationship, the difference between accepting the boy as a friend and acknowledging him as his own son remained a hurdle still to be overcome.

Kit knew that final acceptance had to come from Nathan himself and time was slowly slipping away. As yet Kit hadn't shown Nathan the birth certificate she'd found in the safe-deposit box, which named him as the boy's father.

Convinced in her own mind of the truth of Mark's parentage, she regarded the certificate merely as confirmation, but somehow she doubted it would be enough to satisfy Nathan.

Since their trip into town to the clinic, the opportunity to talk to Nathan alone had rarely presented itself. Either Mark, Joyce or Carmen were somewhere nearby making it impossible for Kit to even broach the subject.

But several times during the past few days Kit had caught Nathan staring at Mark with a look of longing in his eyes, a look he'd quickly suppressed.

It was Saturday evening and Kit and Carmen were washing the supper dishes, chatting about Carmen's date with Bruce. He'd telephoned to invite her on a sleigh ride and Kit could tell by Carmen's sparkling eyes and nervous anticipation that she was looking forward to the outing.

Suddenly Mark came running into the kitchen, his face alight with excitement.

"Want to help decorate the Christmas tree?" he asked as Joyce appeared behind him.

"A Christmas tree? What Christmas tree?" Kit responded.

"The one Nathan cut the other morning and put in the winery to dry off." Joyce turned to Carmen. "Do you think Bruce would mind lending us a hand to bring the tree inside when he comes by to pick you up?" Joyce asked.

"Let's ask." Carmen replied.

Bruce was willing to oblige, trudging down to the main building, and under Kit and Carmen's direction carried the tree to the front of the house, through the foyer and into the sitting room.

Joyce and Mark had already cleared the small nest of tables and the padded Queen Anne chair from the alcove to the right of the fireplace, in order to make room for the tree. Nathan had assembled the tree stand and in no time at all the seven-foot majestic fir stood proudly in the sitting room.

Mark could barely contain his excitement at the prospect of decorating the tree. Prior to Bruce's arrival, Mark and Kit had helped Joyce carry several boxes full of Christmas decorations from a storage cupboard upstairs.

After Carmen and Bruce departed on their date, everyone including Cleo and Piper, returned to the sitting room.

Nathan sat in a chair near the fireplace browsing through the newspaper, but he found his concentration wavering as his thoughts turned to Carmen and Bruce. He was surprised to discover that while he liked and admired Bruce, he was still a little bothered by the fact that a relationship was forming between his friend and his sister-in-law.

Carmen deserved to find happiness again and maybe Kit had been right when she'd said Carmen was obviously ready to move on with her life, ready to leave the past behind.

Nathan glanced surreptitiously over the top of the newspaper at the activity going on on the opposite side of the fireplace. Mark was sitting on the carpet at Joyce's feet helping her string popcorn and cranberries the way he and his brother had done as children. Kit was hanging a string of colored lights on the tree.

During the past few days Nathan had spent a good deal of time with Mark and he'd grown fond of the boy whose sense of fun and adventure, openness and capacity to love, had gone a long way to melt the icy wall around his heart.

Silently Nathan admitted to himself that *if* he had a son of his own, a prospect that seemed remote indeed, he hoped the boy would be like Mark. But he couldn't let his guard down, couldn't allow himself to speculate that Mark might be his, because he knew it wasn't true.

Hurt though he'd been by Angela's betrayal, Nathan hadn't simply allowed her just to walk out of his life. He'd hired a detective to keep tabs on her and every month until the child was born, he'd received a brief report.

The fact that she'd gone to Toronto and not Los Angeles had surprised him, but five months later, and seven months to the day when he'd met her, the report arrived telling him that she'd given birth to a healthy baby boy. That's when he'd finally closed the file on her, that's when he'd learned that the child couldn't possibly have been his. And that's when his heart had turned to ice.

Nathan lifted his gaze from the boy on the rug and watched Kit step up onto the footstool. He let his gaze linger for a moment on her slim ankles and shapely legs and felt his pulse pick up speed as his glance slid upward past the hip-hugging stirrup pants and blue cashmere sweater she wore, coming to a halt at the slender curve of her neck.

As always her hair was twisted into one long tidy braid that almost reached her waist. For a fleeting moment Nathan remembered the erotic feel of her hair on his hands and not for the first time there flashed into his mind an image of Kit lying naked on his bed, her hair cascading across his pillow, her arms reaching out to him.

"Nathan, give Kit a hand, would you?" His mother's words startled him, cutting through his wayward thoughts.

"What...?"

"I said, give Kit a hand with those lights," Joyce repeated, a hint of exasperation in her tone. "You said this morning your ankle was much better."

"It is," he said, setting the paper aside. Thanks to the care and attention he'd received during the past few days the swelling had disappeared. He stood up, feeling only a twinge of pain and leaving the crutch on the floor, crossed the carpet to where Kit was standing on the small stool.

"Here's another string of lights," Mark said as he thrust a set of wires and colored bulbs at Nathan.

Kit kept her attention focused on the task in hand. The shiver of awareness dancing through her told her all too clearly that Nathan was close by.

"Plug this set into the other," he instructed as he handed her the second set of lights.

Kit deliberately avoided touching Nathan as she took the lights from him. She had to stretch up on the tips of her toes in order to connect the two strings. Arms aching from the effort, she finally succeeded in joining them, but as she stepped down off the footstool she suddenly found herself up against Nathan's solid frame.

His arms immediately went around her and at his touch Kit felt her heart kick wildly in her breast.

"Easy does it!" Nathan cautioned, unwilling to take a step back for fear of tripping over Mark, and all the while aware of the cool exotic scent of her invading his senses.

"Sorry!" Kit mumbled, turning slowly in the circle of his arms. As their bodies brushed against each other, a reaction as instantaneous as an explosion sent a flash of desire spiraling through her.

The air between them was suddenly alive with tension and as her gaze flew to meet his, she was in time to see a look of desire glow in the depths of his eyes.

Nathan released Kit and careful to avoid Mark, managed to take a step back, fighting the almost overwhelming urge to do the exact opposite. There was something about this woman that drew him like a magnet and awakened needs he'd long since buried.

Returning to the chair he sat down and retrieved the newspaper from the floor, glad of the rather flimsy protection it afforded. But as he tried to focus on the words in front of him, they made no sense at all. Still swirling in his head was the memory of the way Kit had brushed tantalizingly against him leaving an ache that refused to go away.

Resolutely Nathan reminded himself that both the woman and the boy would be leaving soon, in all probability as early as next week. And once they were gone, he felt sure life would return to normal. But strangely this thought brought neither a feeling of consolation or satisfaction.

"Kit! Why don't you plug those lights in and make sure they're all working before we start putting on the rest of the decorations." The suggestion came from Joyce, and it was with a sense of relief that Kit moved to do as she was asked.

She was still trying to recover from those brief but heart-stopping moments when she'd found herself in Nathan's arms. It was obvious by his cool and nonchalant behavior that he had been unaffected by the encounter, making her wonder if she'd merely imagined the look of desire she'd seen in his eyes.

"They're all lit," Mark said when she plugged in the lights. "Can we put the popcorn strings on now?" he asked Joyce.

"Of course, child," Joyce said with a warm smile.

"Kit, you do the top half and I'll do the bottom half," Mark instructed as he eagerly began to hook the popcorn-and-cranberry string he'd made onto the tree's branches.

"And I'll play Christmas carols," Joyce said as she rose from the love seat and crossed to the piano.

As Joyce began to play the familiar notes of "Silent Night" Kit glanced at Mark who was intent on hanging the colorful ornaments on the tree. A wave of emotion swept over her at the look of pure happiness on Mark's face, and she had to blink back the tears suddenly brimming in her eyes.

As she watched, she silently made her own Christmas wish that they could spend Christmas here, that she could give Mark the kind of Christmas he deserved—Christmas with his family, his father, and his grandmother.

With a sigh Kit pushed her troubles aside and simply gave herself up to enjoying each memory-making moment. Mark's eyes sparkled like the lights on the tree as he worked alongside Kit. Joyce continued to play and Kit soon joined in singing the Christmas carols. Even Nathan succumbed to the magic, lending his low baritone voice to several choruses.

The dogs lay quietly on the carpet, content to be there, only lifting their heads inquisitively when Kit ran upstairs to her room to retrieve her camera. She took a number of snapshots of Mark adding tinsel to the tree and Joyce seated at the piano, even managing to capture Nathan as he put the gold-trimmed angel on top of the tree.

"Kit, Mark and you, too, Nathan. You've done a terrific job. The tree looks absolutely wonderful," said Joyce, a husky note in her voice. She quickly cleared her throat. "Who would like a cup of hot chocolate with marshmallows floating on top?" she added with a bright smile.

"I would! I would!" Mark was the first to respond.

"I'll help," Kit said, and followed Joyce from the room.

"Carmen and I have decorated the tree for the past few years," Joyce said as she put two mugs of milk in the microwave. "Somehow it was always more of a chore than a labor of love. But tonight, having you and Mark here made it special again. I don't think I'll ever forget it," she added and Kit saw the glimmer of tears in the older woman's eyes.

"Neither will we," Kit responded softly.

The quiet moment was suddenly interrupted when the dogs and Mark came running into the kitchen.

"Cleo and Piper want to go out," he told them as they hurried toward the back door.

Later as they sat sipping their hot chocolate in front of the fire Kit let her gaze shift to Nathan. He appeared to be deep in thought, staring into the flickering flames of the gas fire, his elbows resting on his knees.

Kit felt a sharp ache tug at her insides as she stared at his handsome profile. As if sensing he was being watched he lifted his gaze to meet hers and even from across the room Kit glimpsed the look of loneliness that danced briefly in his eyes.

"Look at the time. It's nearly eleven. I'm off to bed," Joyce said, effectively drawing Kit's attention away from Nathan.

"It's way past your bedtime, Mark," Kit said, smiling as she watched him stifle a yawn. "Help me collect the mugs and we'll take them to the kitchen before we go upstairs."

They said their good nights and it wasn't long before Kit was tucking Mark into bed. As she bent to kiss him, he opened his eyes and smiled up at her rather sleepily.

"I wish we could stay here forever," he said on a wistful sigh before he drifted off to sleep.

Kit stood for a long time looking down at Mark. She could easily understand why he wanted to stay, but hearing his wish had caused a pain to stab at her heart.

She drew a steadying breath and reminded herself that she'd made the journey to British Columbia to unite Mark with his father. That Mark would have no objection to staying on was obvious. During the short time they'd been there he'd quickly come to love and accept his new surroundings, due to Joyce Alexander's warmth and generosity.

And Kit couldn't help thinking that it wasn't altogether fair that Joyce should be the only one who didn't know that Mark was her grandson.

Perhaps this was as good a time as any to point this out to Nathan. Perhaps if she showed him the birth certificate... Taking another deep breath Kit crossed to her room and after locating the brown envelope containing Mark's birth certificate and other papers, which had belonged to Angela, she made her way downstairs.

A shaft of light came from beneath the sitting room door and Kit knocked quietly before entering. Nathan was standing in front of the fire with his back to her. He glanced over his shoulder and she noted the look of surprise and something more that flashed in his eyes.

"Forget something?" he asked.

"No, I think we should talk," she said, crossing the carpeted floor toward him.

"I don't see that we have anything to talk about," he said evenly as he turned to face her.

"I brought you this," Kit replied, holding out the envelope.

"What's in it?" Nathan asked as he took it from her.

"Mark's birth certificate," she told him.

"And that's supposed to be positive proof he's my son?" Nathan said as he tossed the envelope onto the love seat.

"You *could* take a look at it," Kit said, sensing his withdrawal, and finding it difficult to curb the impulse to shake him.

"The fact that my name's on the document doesn't necessarily mean that what's written on it is true," he told her. "And before you start in about blood types, I already know that it's possible I could be Mark's father, but it's equally possible that I'm not," he concluded.

Kit stared in stunned silence at him. That he knew about the birth certificate was obvious but that he was also cognizant of the inconclusive evidence of the matching blood types came as a complete surprise.

"But how..." Kit began, scarcely able to believe what she'd heard.

"A week after Angela walked out I called a detective agency in Vancouver and asked them to locate her," Nathan said with a sigh. "I told them I thought she'd probably gone back to L.A. that I just wanted to confirm it," he continued. "When they called a week later to say she was staying with two other models in Toronto, I was a bit surprised, but I assumed she'd gone there on a modeling job.

"They told me if I wanted to keep her under surveillance they'd give me the number of a private detective in Toronto. I called and instructed him to keep a perfunctory eye on Angela and to send me a report every month until the baby was born."

Kit heard the pain and resignation in Nathan's voice and her heart went out to him. She was warmed by the knowledge that hurt and disillusioned as he must have been at the time, he'd still been concerned enough for Angela's welfare to make sure she was all right.

It was difficult to stay angry at him and at his stubborn refusal to accept Mark as his son, especially when she knew that Angela had been the one at fault, the one who'd deliberately lied to Nathan about the child she was carrying.

Not once as Angela lay dying had she offered any explanation as to the reason for her lies. Right or wrong Kit could only speculate, but recalling how Joyce had made mention of the fact that after returning with his new wife, Nathan had been kept busy with the annual harvesting of the grapes, and Kit wondered now if Angela, accustomed to being the center of attention, had grown to resent the time Nathan spent away from her.

Knowing Angela's love for the city, for the noise, action and excitement that was part and parcel of most large metropolises, Kit wondered if having found herself in such a rugged, out of way part of British Columbia, Angela had not adjusted well to her new surroundings and possibly found the area much too isolated.

"Marry in haste, repent at leisure." The old phrase certainly seemed appropriate, Kit thought with a sigh. But somehow it didn't seem fair that Mark should be the one to suffer, that because of Angela's selfishness, a child like Mark should be deprived of the only family he had left in the world.

"Jamieson's final report arrived less than five months later," Kit heard Nathan say, effectively bringing her attention back to the man standing nearby. She frowned. Jamieson? The name seemed somehow familiar...she was almost sure she'd seen it written somewhere amid Angela's papers. But before she could pursue the thought further, Nathan continued.

"In it he wrote that Angela had given birth to a baby boy, weighing in at eight pounds ten ounces. He even enclosed a copy of the birth certificate, but I really didn't need to read any more. The child was born exactly seven months from the day I met Angela and I knew there was no possible way he could be mine, which meant she had to have been pregnant when I met her."

Kit said nothing, silently digesting this information. Something was out of whack but she couldn't put her finger on it. Nathan appeared to have covered all the bases and much as she might have wanted to argue the matter she wasn't foolish enough to suggest that the birth might have been premature, not with Mark weighing in at almost nine pounds.

"Cat got your tongue, Miss Bellamy?" Nathan asked, but there was no sarcasm in his tone, and lifting her gaze to meet his, Kit instantly saw the look of sorrow and regret in his eyes. He'd wanted to believe her, she saw that as clearly as if he'd spoken the words aloud, but the evidence he'd uncovered before she and Mark had even arrived on the scene had been stacked against her, undermining her efforts and making her journey not only futile but totally unnecessary.

"No! It's just not true," Kit said, surprising herself with the intensity of her feelings. "You *are* Mark's father. Why would Angela lie to me? What would be the point? She was dying!" Something was definitely haywire, Kit felt it in her bones.

"Damn it, woman!" Nathan almost shouted the words as he took a step toward her. "Haven't you been listening to a word I said?"

As his hands came up to clasp her upper arms the expression on his handsome features was a mixture of exasperation and anger. For a fleeting moment Kit thought he was going to shake her, just as she'd wanted to shake him a little while ago, but almost immediately his touch gentled and as he continued his tone changed to one of hollow resignation. "You did what you thought was right, and I applaud you for that. But no matter how much we both might want it to be true, Mark isn't my son."

Kit felt her heart shudder to a standstill then pick up speed once more. "But why didn't you tell me this when we arrived?" she asked.

Nathan sighed. "You arrived the day the storm hit. How could I turn you away?" he answered evenly. "And I admit, at first, well... you seemed so damned sure of yourself that I found myself wondering if there might have been something I missed, that you might really have some evidence...." He ground to a halt and drew a ragged breath, dropping his hands to his sides. "Later, as I watched the way my mother took to Mark... the way her face lit up whenever he was around—" He broke off, emotion clogging his voice now. "I know how much a grandchild would mean to her...."

Kit heard the pain and longing in his voice, glimpsed the sadness shadowing his eyes and instinctively her hand came up to touch him in a gesture solely meant to comfort.

At the contact a jolt, not unlike a small electric shock, scampered up her arm and for a startling moment their eyes met and held. Kit's breath caught in her throat at the desire that flared to life in the depths of Nathan's eyes.

Her vision blurred as he began to close the gap between them, and her heart beat out a thunderous tattoo against her breast in heady anticipation of his mouth touching hers.

Suddenly the door behind them opened. "I hope you weren't waiting up for me.... Oh... sorry!" Carmen's voice cut through the shimmering tension and Kit and Nathan sprang apart like two teenagers caught kissing on the couch.

"It's all right...." Nathan and Kit spoke at the same instant and Kit felt her face grow hot with embarrassment.

"I saw the light under the door," Carmen said, glancing from Kit to Nathan and back again, a questioning look on her face.

"How was your date with Bruce?" Kit asked, managing to smile as she moved away from Nathan.

"We had a wonderful time," Carmen said on a sigh, her face aglow at the mention of Bruce. "Oh, by the way," she quickly went on. "I was telling Bruce about you growing up near Peachville and how Joyce thought Tobias might remember your parents and where you lived. Anyway, he said he saw Tobias yesterday, and that the Sheridans are back from L.A." She stopped and turned to Nathan. "You should give them a call and take Kit over there."

A shiver of excitement danced through Kit at the prospect of meeting and talking to Tobias Sheridan. She glanced at Nathan, noting the rather thoughtful expression on his face.

"I'll call Drew first thing tomorrow morning," he said. "But right now, if you'll excuse me, I'll let the dogs out for a brief sojourn and then head to bed. Good night."

"'Night," Carmen and Kit echoed as Nathan made his way from the sitting room.

"I'm sorry if I interrupted..." Carmen began.

"No, actually it was probably for the best," Kit quickly responded.

"I gather that you haven't succeeded in changing his mind about Mark," Carmen said.

Kit shook her head. There was little point in explaining to Carmen what had happened, and now in view of the news she had brought of the Sheridans return, Kit was suddenly faced with the realization that once she spoke to Tobias, once she had garnered what little, if any, information he might have about her parents, there would no longer be any reason for her and Mark to stay on.

Chapter Eleven

Kit lay in bed unable to sleep. Her thoughts kept returning to the confrontation in the sitting room with Nathan. Though she tried to make sense of all that he'd told her, she was constantly being distracted by the question of just what would have happened if Carmen hadn't arrived when she did.

Kit stirred restlessly beneath the covers knowing she was merely fooling herself. She knew exactly what would have happened and how she would have responded had Nathan kissed her. Just thinking about his mouth touching hers made her insides turn to jelly, and not for the first time she wondered at the devastating effect he had on her senses.

Resolutely she refused to analyze or explore the reasons behind her turbulent emotions, and tried instead to concentrate on the details of the story Nathan had recounted of how he'd tracked Angela to Toronto.

Even after the evidence Nathan had parleyed, Kit was still sure in her heart that Nathan was Mark's father. The conviction that some vital piece of information was missing continued to plague her. The detective's name had seemed familiar, but try as she might to recall in what context, Kit could think of no explanation. Stymied she eventually drifted off into a troubled sleep.

It came as something of a surprise when she awakened the next morning to discover that it was well past nine o'clock. Pushing the covers aside she crossed to Mark's room but there was no sign of her young charge.

Glancing around she could tell by the way he'd haphazardly made his bed and tossed his pajamas on top, that he'd dressed in a hurry. She guessed that he was either with Nathan or Joyce and knowing that time spent with them was fast running out, Kit saw no need to hurry.

With a sigh she gathered her toiletry bag and some items of clothing and made her way to the bathroom.

Half an hour later, her hair carefully twisted into a French braid and wearing navy slacks and a cowl-necked midnight-blue sweater, Kit descended the stairs and crossed to the kitchen.

Joyce greeted her with a smile. "Good morning, my dear. In case you're wondering Mark is with Nathan and Carmen. They took the dogs for a walk."

"Nathan's ankle must be much better," Kit said as she poured herself a cup of coffee.

"Yes, it is," Joyce acknowledged. "He's isn't limping at all today. Now, what can I get you for breakfast?"

"Toast would be just fine," Kit replied. "I'm afraid I slept in. But, please, I can manage. I don't expect you to wait on me."

"That's all right," Joyce assured her. "It's Sunday and everyone's entitled to sleep in on a Sunday morning."

"What about you? Did you sleep late?" Kit asked.

Joyce shook her head and smiled. "Not me. I'm awake every morning at exactly seven o'clock," she told Kit. "I don't remember the last time I slept in. Habit, I suppose, but not one that I'm liable to break anytime soon. Oh, by the way, Nathan telephoned Drew Sheridan this morning and explained that you'd like to talk to Tobias. Drew was kind enough to invite us to drop over this afternoon."

Kit felt her pulse skip a beat.

"I'm so looking forward to seeing Vienna and the boys." Joyce crossed to the fridge. "They are such a nice family," she added as she brought out a small pitcher of cream.

Kit set her cup on the counter, unsure where the feeling of panic suddenly racing through her had sprouted from. "But are you sure they don't mind? I mean ... if they've been away, they must be busy making preparations for Christmas. I wouldn't want to intrude."

Joyce gazed at her, a surprised expression on her face. "But, my dear, I thought ..." she began then stopped, a look of sympathy and understanding coming into her eyes. "I assure you they're looking forward to meeting you," she said gently. "I think you'll like Vienna. She's one of the nicest, kindest people I know," Joyce went on. "She lost her parents, too, you know."

Kit blinked away the tears suddenly threatening to overwhelm her. She hadn't realized just how much finding out where she'd once lived as a child, or discovering more about the parents she'd loved and lost so long ago had actually meant to her, until now.

Yet a part of her was afraid, afraid of being disappointed, of coming away empty-handed, of arriving at the Sheridans only to be told by Tobias that he didn't remember her parents and could tell her nothing.

"I'm sorry..." Kit mumbled, swallowing the lump in her throat.

"Don't apologize, child. I quite understand," Joyce said gently. "But, believe me, Tobias has a good memory. If your parents lived anywhere in the area he'll either have known them, or know someone who did."

Before Kit could reply the back door opened and the dogs came running in followed by Mark, Carmen and Nathan. Kit drew a steadying breath before she turned to greet them and as her gaze lit on Nathan she felt her heart stumble against her breast in an all too familiar response.

"Good morning! How was your walk?" she asked in a cheery voice, lowering her gaze now to Mark.

"Super," came the prompt reply, his cheeks aglow from the outing.

"I'm sorry I missed it," Kit said. "Why didn't you wake me?"

"Nathan said not to," Mark explained, flashing a smile at the man beside him.

Kit's eyes flew to meet Nathan's. Surely he hadn't come into her bedroom? The thought sent a shiver of awareness chasing through her.

Kit noted the flash of amusement and something more that appeared in the depths of Nathan's eyes before he spoke. "Mark and I ran into each other in the hallway," he explained, almost as if he'd read her mind, "and when he said you weren't awake yet, I suggested he let you sleep."

"Oh, I see," said Kit, not sure now whether to be relieved or disappointed.

"Mother, did you tell Kit about our invitation to the Sheridans this afternoon?" Nathan asked as he helped himself to a cup from the cupboard and filled it from the coffeepot.

"I just did," Joyce replied as the telephone rang.

"That'll be for me," Carmen said as she reached for the receiver on the counter nearby. "Hello! Yes, just a minute," she said before lowering the receiver to the counter. "It's Bruce. I'll get out of everybody's way and take the call upstairs," she added, her eyes sparkling. "Would you hang it up for me?"

"Of course," Nathan replied as Carmen hurried from the kitchen.

Joyce smiled after the departing figure. "I haven't seen Carmen this happy in a long time," she said.

"She deserves to be happy," Nathan said as he quietly replaced the receiver.

"Everyone deserves a little happiness," his mother countered. "The trick is to recognize it, then reach out and grab it before it passes you by," she added in a quiet matter-of-fact tone of voice, making Kit glance at the older woman, but Joyce had already turned away.

They set out for Peachville immediately after lunch. Nathan drove, confirming that his injury was more or less a thing of the past. Joyce sat next to her son, while Kit and Mark occupied the back seat.

To no one's surprise Carmen informed them Bruce was picking her up later and they'd be out for the afternoon and evening. Cleo and Piper were left in charge and as Nathan took the turn onto the highway, Kit felt her stomach tighten in anticipation of the afternoon ahead.

The journey to Peachville was completed in a little over thirty-five minutes. Beside her, Mark busied himself drawing pictures and Kit spent most of the time gazing out at the snow-covered landscape scanning the roads and houses they passed wondering if she might catch a glimpse of the house where she'd once lived.

As Nathan brought the van to a halt at the top of the Sheridans' driveway, the front door of the house opened and out bounded a golden retriever followed by a small white poodle.

"Wow! Kit, look! Isn't he beautiful?" Mark said when he spotted the retriever heading toward the van. He began to fumble with his seat belt eager to greet the dogs.

Kit smiled as she released her own seat belt and turned to assist Mark. Glancing at the house she saw a young woman with a small child in her arms standing in the open doorway smiling and waving as they emerged from the van.

"Hi, there! We've been watching for you. Come on in," she called to them.

Already out of the van, Mark was being welcomed by the two dogs who were jumping around him wagging their tails as if he was a long-lost friend.

"Take my arm," Nathan said to his mother, and with Kit, Mark and the dogs bringing up the rear they made their way along the shoveled walkway.

"Joyce, Nathan, it's wonderful to see you," the young woman at the door said as they approached.

"Vienna, you look radiant as usual," Joyce commented as she kissed Vienna's cheek.

"And you must be Kit and Mark. I'm so pleased you could come," Vienna said with a friendly smile. "This is Kade," she told them smiling at the boy in her arms. "Let's get in out of the cold. Come on through to the kitchen and I'll take your coats. Buffy, Rags, settle down you two," she told the dogs in a firm voice.

"Where's Drew?" Nathan asked as they followed Vienna into the large spacious kitchen.

"He's up in the attic with Chris. I sent them up there to find and bring down the Christmas decorations," she explained before kissing Kade and setting him down in the center of a small playpen nearby. "There, my lad, it's almost nap time, but you can play with your toys for a little while," she told him. "Now, give me your coats." She turned to her guests once more. "Ah, darling, there you are..." she added, her pretty face lighting up like a beacon when a tall dark-haired man appeared in the doorway.

"It looks and sounds like Grand Central Station in here," the man said as he came forward to shake hands with Nathan. "Hey, buddy, how's it going?" he asked.

After introductions and handshakes all around it was several minutes before the noise died down and in the interim Kit and Mark met Vienna's husband, Drew, her ten-year-old stepson, Chris, and her father-in-law, Tobias Sheridan.

Kit quickly felt at ease in the warm and friendly atmosphere and immediately took a liking to the slender, attractive, young woman who was Joyce Alexander's friend.

"Do you want to see the puppies?" Chris asked Mark and at his question Mark's eyes widened in wonder.

"Puppies?" Mark repeated breathlessly.

"Our dog Daisy had eight puppies six weeks ago," said Chris proudly. "We keep them in a room at the back," he explained. "They'll be leaving us soon 'cause Vienna has found homes for all except two of them," he told Mark. "Come on I'll show you," he added and without further ado the boys hurried off.

Moments later Drew hauled Nathan off to his office for a man-to-man chat.

"Tobias, why don't you take Kit into the living room and while you talk, Joyce and I can catch up on all that's happened around here since we've been away in California," Vienna suggested a few minutes later.

"Good idea," said Tobias. "Don't forget to plug in the kettle. I could sure use a cup of tea." He winked at his daughter-in-law.

Kit felt tears prick her eyes at the love that was so abundant in this house. For a moment she found herself envying Vienna the happiness that seemed to emanate from every member of the family.

"Sit down, my dear, and tell me what you remember," Tobias said as he ushered Kit through to the living room and lowered himself into a comfortable old easy chair by the fire.

Kit sat down across from Tobias. Gathering her thoughts together she took a steadying breath before she spoke. "My parents moved to this area when I was just a baby," she began. "My father's name was Michael Bellamy, he was a cabinetmaker," she told him softly. "My mother's name was Elizabeth and she was a dressmaker." She stopped and lifted her gaze to the man seated opposite.

"Go on," he said, his tone encouraging, his smile reassuring.

"My memory of the cottage is rather sketchy. It was quite small," Kit said. "There was a living room, kitchen and bathroom on the main floor and two bedrooms upstairs. My bedroom was very tiny and my parents' bedroom wasn't much bigger," she recalled. "My mother set her sewing machine up in the living room and I can remember sitting on the floor playing while she worked. I think my father had a work shed outside, but I'm not sure. We didn't go out much. My father owned a small boat, which he'd built and he and my mother liked to go fishing. The only people who ever came to the house were customers. Either for my mother's sewing or for my father's cabinetwork."

"Do you remember going to school?" Tobias asked.

Kit shook her head. "I didn't go to school. It was too far away, at least that's what my father said. So my mother taught me to read and write at home, she used to work with me every morning, then in the afternoon she would sew," Kit said, her voice wavering a little as she spoke. "Do you remember them?" Kit asked, unable to hold back the question any longer.

Tobias smiled kindly at her. "I was a little surprised when Vienna told me your name and the reason you wanted to talk to me. I had to cast my mind back a good twenty years, but the first thing I recalled was reading in the paper about the boating accident..." He stopped and threw her a concerned glance.

"It's all right," she quietly assured him. "Please, go on..." she urged, her hopes still high.

Tobias nodded. "Over the years I've often wondered what became of you."

"You knew me? Then you must have known my parents," Kit said and felt her heart skip a beat.

"As much as anyone around here knew them," Tobias answered evenly. "They were private people, they kept to themselves, didn't socialize much at all, but simply went about their business quietly and efficiently."

"Oh, so you didn't actually meet them..." Kit's initial elation was waning fast.

"I met them," he quietly assured her. "And if my memory serves me well, I met you, too, the day I dropped by to pick up a night table I had your father make for me. Unfortunately I don't have it now."

"You met me? Really? I don't remember..." She was babbling but she couldn't seem to stop as a mixture of excitement and exhilaration shot through her. "So you must know where the cottage is located? Is it far? Is it still there?" The questions popping into her head were coming fast and furious.

"Yes, it's still there, and strangely enough it's vacant at the moment," Tobias told her. "Probably because it's in need of repair. The last tenants moved out back in September, I believe. Ah, Vienna you brought us a pot of tea, thank you, my dear," he added as she set a tray on the coffee table in front of them.

"Is there enough in the pot for Nathan and me?" The question came from Drew who'd appeared from the hallway with Nathan close behind.

"Of course," Vienna said flashing her husband a smile. "Are the boys still in with the puppies?" she asked.

"Yes," Drew replied. "I peeked in on Kade, he's fast asleep."

"Good. I'll just bring a cup for each of you. And if all is quiet on the western front, Joyce and I might as well join you, too," she added before slipping from the room.

Kit silently accepted the cup of tea Tobias held out to her. She was still trying to deal with the fact that he had actually known her parents and was familiar with the cottage where she'd once lived. While she'd appreciated Joyce's enthusiasm in wanting her to meet Tobias, Kit hadn't really expected that he would remember her parents. She hadn't wanted to get her hopes up too high...but now...

As Nathan sat down on the long low chesterfield he noted the rather dazed look on Kit's face.

"Were you able to help Kit track down the cottage where she lived?" he asked Tobias.

"Yes, as a matter of fact I was," Tobias said, before taking a sip of tea. "You know it, too, Nathan. It's that tiny cottage set back off the road a good ten miles down the highway. The one past old Dan Ashton's place," Tobias continued.

"Dan still owns it, doesn't he?" Drew jumped in. "Jake Russell and his wife, Susie, rented it from him for a while before they bought a house in that brand-new development on the other side of town."

Nathan frowned and nodded. He knew the cottage they were talking about, and it wasn't far away. "We could take a drive over there right now," he suggested and at his words Kit's gaze flew to his and he saw the look of appreciation as well as apprehension glinting in her eyes.

"Now there's an idea," Tobias said. "You could even make a stop at the cemetery, it's on the way. We'd come along with you but I believe the boss has a job lined up for us menfolk..." he said, motioning with his head toward the doorway as Vienna and Joyce appeared.

"That's right," said Vienna. "In a house with four males someone has to take charge," she countered, humor lacing her voice as she moved to stand next to her husband near the upright piano.

"You did say you wanted to put the Christmas tree up today, didn't you?" Drew said teasingly, putting his arm around his wife.

"That was the order for the day," Vienna replied, leaning into the man beside her, smiling warmly at him. "But if you think it's too much for you..." Her words trailed off then she turned to Kit. "You know, it's getting harder and harder to find good help these days," Vienna continued on an exaggerated sigh. "I'm seriously considering trading in these two...."

Drew swooped down and silenced his wife with a kiss, as laughter broke out around them.

"What was that you were saying, my love?" Drew asked a moment later.

Vienna laughed, too. "I think I've forgotten," she said, her smile full of love.

Watching the brief exchange, Nathan felt as he always did when he visited his friends, how lucky Drew and Vienna were to be so much in love. He envied them their happiness, their obvious joy in each other.

"Would you like to come with us, Mother?" Nathan asked as he stood up.

"No, thank you, dear. I'll stay and keep Vienna company," she said. "You might as well leave Mark here. He'll be fine with Chris and the puppies."

"I'll get the boys to give us a hand to bring in the tree, later," Drew suggested.

"Thank you . . . you've all been so kind . . ." Kit managed to say, emotion clogging her throat.

"Let's go," Nathan said and with that they headed to the door.

Kit sat in the passenger seat watching the passing countryside. They'd stopped at the cemetery for a few minutes, and with Nathan's help she'd located the headstones, but as she placed two small holly wreaths Vienna had given her on the snow-covered ground Kit could garner little emotion for the place.

Nathan had been silent since they'd set out from the Sheridans' and for that Kit was appreciative. A mixture of apprehension and anticipation was making her heart beat a rapid tattoo inside her chest, and her stomach, too, was dipping and rising almost as if she were riding on a roller coaster.

Not until Nathan reached over and covered her hands briefly with one of his did she realize she was clutching her gloves in a viselike grip.

At the contact a shiver ran through her and she threw him a startled glance. Their eyes met and held for a fleeting moment and in that second of time Kit felt her anxiety ease and a calmness wash over her.

A few minutes later Nathan turned the van into a narrow driveway hidden by a high hedgerow and immediately brought the van to a halt.

"We'll leave the van here and walk up the driveway," Nathan said as he shut off the engine and reached for the door handle.

Kit hardly heard what he said, she was staring at the tiny cottage nestled behind the hedgerow. Her breath caught in her throat and her eyes filled with moisture as she recognized the quaint but small dwelling where she had lived as a child.

When the passenger door beside her opened she turned to find Nathan smiling encouragingly at her.

"The snow's pretty deep, but it's soft and powdery," he told her as he held out his hand to help her down.

Kit quickly blinked back the tears and pulling on her gloves accepted Nathan's hand.

"Stay behind me. I'll forge a path," he told her, flashing a smile as he moved off in the direction of the cottage.

Kit had no difficulty keeping up with him, eager now to reach the front porch. An old corn broom stood against the wall and Nathan soon swept the powdered snow from the doorway.

"I bet there's a key hidden around here somewhere," he said as he put the broom back.

Kit didn't respond; she couldn't. Memories of her childhood, memories she'd locked away in a private corner of her heart slowly began to surface.

"Here we are," Nathan said, showing her the key he'd found, before turning to unlock the front door.

Kit closed her eyes and held her breath, allowing herself a fanciful thought, that when the door opened she would see her parents.

Her heart skidded to a halt when she heard the creak of the door, but reality enveloped her when she opened her eyes to find herself gazing into a bare living room.

"Would you like me to leave you alone?" Nathan's softly spoken question brought her attention away from the cold and dismal interior of the house.

"No, please stay," she managed to say as she fought back the tears suddenly threatening to overflow. Her throat ached from the effort not to cry and it was all she could do to take that first step across the threshold.

Nathan instantly moved to Kit's side and put his arm around her. That she was bravely trying to cope with what must for her be an incredibly emotional moment was obvious by the rigid tension in her body, the paleness of her features and the tears shimmering in her gray-green eyes.

He felt strangely protective toward this woman who had stormed into his life a week ago to create havoc, awakening needs he'd long since buried, and challenging him to put the past behind him and get on with his life.

She had a sense of pride and determination, and a strength of character no man could dismiss or ignore. Even in this extraordinary situation, when most people would simply fall apart, she was grimly trying to hold herself together.

They crossed the threshold and not knowing what else to do Nathan slowly walked her through the rooms on the main floor saying nothing, unwilling to intrude, simply giving her the time to assimilate and deal with her emotions.

A procession of memories, jumbled and confused enveloped Kit. Images of her mother standing in the kitchen near the stove, crouched over her sewing machine, or gently brushing the tangles from her hair flashed into Kit's head. Pictures of her father's smiling face as he greeted them each afternoon when he came through the front door bombarded her mind and her heart.

Nathan's presence, both physically and emotionally gave Kit the strength she needed to face her memories, memories she'd shut away, memories that had been too painful to explore and examine until now.

They had completed a circuit of the main floor, returning once more to the tiny living room. Kit deliberately slowed to a halt and smiled sadly to herself as a fresh stream of memories surfaced causing first one tear then another to spill over and trace a path down her cheek.

Without a word Nathan urged her gently but firmly into the secure haven of his arms and as the sobs tore through her he simply held her close till the storm raging inside gradually began to subside.

Slowly, miraculously, her sorrow spent, Kit felt a sense of peace and tranquility steal over her, easing the pain in her heart, leaving in its wake the feelings of love and happiness she'd associated with her parents and this cottage.

"Better now?" Nathan's voice was little more than a whisper, and Kit nodded, reluctant to leave the warmth and security of his arms.

She lifted her head from his shoulder. "I'm sorry..." she began.

"Don't be," he said softly, as he pulled a handkerchief from his pocket and with delicate care wiped the wetness from her cheeks.

"I guess we should go," Kit said, noticing now that the room had grown dark.

"I guess we should," Nathan said, his breath fanning her face causing a shiver to chase through her. But he made no move to release her.

Kit lifted her eyes to meet his gaze and saw the look of torment that flickered in the depths of his eyes a mere second before his mouth came down unerringly on hers.

His kiss was achingly sweet and infinitely tender, offering only comfort at a time when she needed it most, chasing away the last remnants of her sorrow and soothing her troubled soul.

And it was during those touchingly powerful moments that she made a startling discovery. This was where she wanted to spend the rest of her life, here in the arms of this sensitive, caring, and sometimes stubborn man.

Though she wasn't sure exactly when or how it had happened, she suddenly knew with every fiber of her being, that she was hopelessly, irrevocably and deeply in love with Nathan Alexander.

Chapter Twelve

Kit felt her heart kick into high gear as she acknowledged the wondrous emotion coursing through her. Her blood began to hum a song of celebration as it sped through her veins carrying the message of love to every cell. She felt more alive, more aware of her own sensuality than at any time in her life and it had everything to do with this man who was holding her so tenderly, so lovingly.

This was wrong! All wrong! Nathan silently chided himself. He shouldn't be kissing her, not when she was so vulnerable. His mother had mentioned to him that her parents had drowned in a boating accident when Kit was a child and he could only imagine how devastating the loss had been.

Coming here had obviously brought back painful memories and he couldn't blame her for releasing all her pent-up sorrow. He was thankful he'd been here to offer comfort, but now wasn't the time to explore the emotions she so easily aroused in him. Right now she simply needed a friend.

Nathan broke the kiss and held Kit away from him. "I'm sorry. That was a mistake," he said and at his words Kit felt as if he'd thrust a dagger into her heart.

"I suppose it was," she managed to say, her voice husky with emotion, her throat aching from the effort to hold back the fresh batch of tears that had gathered behind her eyes.

"We should be getting back," Nathan said, his breath forming a white cloud as he moved away. "It's freezing in here. I'll go and warm up the van and wait for you there." He stopped in the doorway and turned to her. "The key's still in the lock. Just put it on the ledge above the door when you leave."

"Thank you," Kit said hugging her arms around her as Nathan closed the front door behind him.

She was relieved to be alone. She needed to collect her thoughts and regain control of her wayward emotions. During the past hour she'd run the gamut as far as her emotions were concerned, ranging from the low of lows, sorrow and despair, to the ultimate high, the realization that she was truly and deeply in love.

She released a long shaky sigh and watched as the cloud of vapor lingered for a moment then dissipated. She hugged herself tighter trying to generate some warmth, but the chilly air seemed to penetrate to her very soul and she wondered if she'd ever feel warm again.

Glancing around the room one last time, she managed a smile as a collage of pictures of her parents flashed into her head. This day would remain forever in her memory as the day she found both peace and love.

By the time she trudged through the snow to the van, Kit's fingers and feet were numb with cold. As Nathan reversed out of the driveway and they began the return journey, the warmth from the van's heater soon chased the chill from her body, but not from her heart.

The snowy landscape shimmered in the early moonlight and as they covered the last mile, they passed several houses, brightly lit with colorful Christmas lights. As the Sheridan house came into view Kit saw that their roof and front windows were outlined with green and red lights that twinkled merrily at them.

They'd hardly spoken a word throughout the drive and Kit couldn't help feeling that the silence between them was awkward rather than companionable.

Nathan brought the van to a halt and switching off the engine he turned to Kit.

"Ready to face the crowd?" he asked and Kit was glad that the van's interior was dark and Nathan couldn't see the tears that sprang to her eyes when she heard the concern in his voice.

She managed to nod, and a few moments later Nathan led her up the back stairs to the kitchen door. The dogs, undoubtedly hearing their approach, began to bark, and pinning on a smile, Kit knocked lightly before entering.

Vienna, the three boys and the dogs were all in the kitchen. Mark, in anticipation of her appearance, was already halfway out of the chair where he'd been sitting, and Kit noted the look of excitement in his eyes.

"Kit, you should see the puppies. There's eight of them, all black, just like Daisy. This is Daisy," he added excitedly as he patted the black lab who'd appeared beside him.

"And hello to you, too," Nathan said, smiling down at the boy, a hint of laughter in his voice.

"Hello you two," Vienna greeted them as she turned from the stove. "We were beginning to wonder if you'd gotten lost," she added with a teasing smile. "Take off your jackets and give them to Chris. He'll take them upstairs. By the way, dinner's almost ready," she went on easily. "Mark and Chris promised me they'd help decorate the tree afterward," she explained.

"Oh, fine," said Kit, turning to Mark who was tugging insistently at her hand.

"Want to see the puppies?" he asked. "They're in the back room," he told her.

"The boys have been playing with the puppies since you left," Vienna explained, wiping her hands on her apron.

"Come and see them," Mark urged again. "See, Daisy wants to show you," he said as the black lab turned and trotted off.

Kit threw Vienna a questioning glance, worried that barging in on the puppies might upset them.

"She's hoping you'll take one home with you," Vienna said. "Daisy's a wonderful mother," she continued. "But I think she'll be quite happy to see her brood go to their new homes. My partner looked after them at the clinic while we were gone, but they're getting to be quite a handful, that's why I try to keep them in the back room," she explained, smiling down at Kade who was tugging at her skirt.

Mark took Kit's hand and led her to a door that opened off the kitchen. A bevy of black shapes came running from all directions and Kit immediately crouched to pat the black bundles of fur.

"Oh, Daisy, they're lovely," Kit said, stroking the puppies who were clamoring for attention, thinking all the while that she'd love to take all eight of them home with her.

Mark was in his element, his face one enormous smile as he gathered two wriggling pups into his arms. "Aren't they super?'' he said. "Chris and Kade are so lucky,'' he added with a sigh, then giggled as one of the puppies energetically began to lick his face.

"They're certainly a lively litter,'' said Nathan from the doorway. "You have your hands... I mean paws full, Daisy,'' he added laughingly as he bent to scoop up one of the puppies trying to escape.

"Do you think Santa got my letter?'' Mark suddenly asked, and Kit felt her heart leap into her throat when she saw the hope and longing in the boy's blue eyes.

"I really don't know,'' she said at last, unwilling to give him false hope, trying with difficulty to keep her tone light, realizing again just how disappointed he was going to be on Christmas morning.

"Time to wash up for supper,'' said Vienna from the doorway. "Come on, Daisy, round 'em up,'' she said.

"Watch this,'' Mark said as he set down the puppies and began to retreat to the door.

Kit followed Mark's lead and watched as Daisy gave a soft but commanding bark then trotted to the far corner where an old quilt was spread out on the floor. She stood there for several moments continuing to "talk" to her children. Obediently they all crossed to the quilt, all except one, who turned and headed straight for Mark, who beamed as he picked up the naughty puppy.

"He did that last time, too,'' Vienna said with a shake of her head as she took the pup from Mark's arms. "I guess he must like you, Mark. We call him Rascal, because he's always getting into mischief,'' she added as she set the pup on the floor and nudged him in the direction of his brothers and sisters.

It took several tries and much laughter before they succeeded in closing in the puppies once more. Kit entered the living room to find Tobias and Joyce chatting by the fire.

In the corner by the window stood a large pine tree, filling the room with its aromatic scent.

"Ah, there you are," said Joyce with a warm smile. "How did it go?" she asked, a look of both curiosity and concern in her eyes.

"Very well, thank you," Kit said, crossing to sit on the chesterfield. "We stopped at the cemetery first, then continued on to the cottage," she told them evenly. "Nathan managed to find a key and we went inside."

"Did you recognize it when you saw it?" Tobias asked.

"Yes...yes, I did..." she said, her voice trembling just a little as her memories threatened to crowd in on her once more.

"I see you have a good eye for picking out the perfect tree, Tobias," Nathan said, shifting topics.

"Considering I have several fields to pick and choose from, it isn't difficult," Tobias replied.

"Excuse me, folks," Drew said as he appeared in the doorway. "If you would all kindly make your way to the dining room. Dinner is served," he announced.

The evening was one of the happiest Kit had spent for a long time. Fun and love and laughter appeared to be the meal's main ingredients, though the food itself was equally superb.

The fact that she was seated directly across from Nathan proved a mixture of heaven and hell for Kit. Their hands continually made fleeting contact as they passed platters back and forth, sending gentle ripples of sensation through her. And each time her gaze met his, a look she couldn't quite decipher flashed briefly in the depths of his eyes.

Kit quietly watched and listened to the happy sounds of animated conversation and genuine laughter going on around the table, storing this memory with all the others she'd collected over the past week.

"Joyce tells me you and Mark are heading back to England soon," Drew said, effectively bringing Kit out of her reverie.

"Yes," she responded, aware that Nathan was watching her closely.

"I wish we didn't have to go," Mark suddenly piped up from the other end of the table. "I wish we could stay here forever," he added wistfully.

Kit heard the longing in Mark's voice, echoing her own feelings on the matter. "I'm not sure we haven't outstayed our welcome as it is," she said, struggling to keep her tone light, while inside her heart felt as if it was slowly being torn apart.

"We've enjoyed having you, my dear," Joyce was quick to assure her. "I know it sounds silly but you and Mark have fitted in like family," she said sincerely.

Kit glanced across the table at Nathan noting the tension in the taut line of his jaw.

"Thank you," Kit managed to say, thinking of the irony of Joyce's words. "Mark and I will never forget your kindness or your hospitality," she added.

"Who wants home-baked apple pie and ice cream?" Vienna asked, pushing her chair back, effectively restoring everyone's smiles.

"I do! I do!" came the boys chorus and soon the chatter of voices around the table resumed.

Later while Drew put Kade to bed and the boys undertook the task of decorating the tree under the watchful eyes of Nathan, Tobias and Joyce, Kit helped Vienna with the dishes.

As they worked companionably together, the two women exchanged thoughts and ideas covering numerous subjects as they sowed the seeds of friendship. When Kit told Vienna of her plans to go into business for herself and open up a photography studio when she returned to England, Vienna was supportive and encouraging.

"It's too bad you're not staying on," she commented. "We could use a photography studio around here. I'm sure it would be a huge success. New families are moving into the area all the time and when you have youngsters it's nice to have a record of their growing up years. They grow up so darned fast these days."

"You certainly keep busy," Kit said. "Joyce told me you're the local vet. It must be hard running a business and looking after a young family..."

"Yes, it is. But Drew is wonderful," Vienna said, love for the man who was her husband echoing in her voice. "I sold half my practice to a friend who went to veterinary school with me. That made things a lot easier for me, especially when Kade was born."

"Mark and I found some more dishes," Chris said as he and Mark joined them in the kitchen.

"Oh, and I thought I was all finished, thanks a lot," Vienna said with a teasing grin, taking a cup and saucer from each of the boys.

Chris headed back to the living room but Mark lingered and it wasn't difficult to guess that he wanted to visit the puppies.

Vienna lowered the last of the dishes into the soapy water. "Kade was born six weeks premature." She continued with her story. "The staff at the hospital were great. They said he was their first 'preemie,' but even then he was hardly that, weighing in at almost five pounds."

"I was preemie, too," Mark said out of the blue.

"You were?" Vienna replied, turning to smile at him.

Mark nodded. "But I weighed nearly four pounds. That's what my mom told me," he said. "Can I go and play with the puppies?" he asked.

"Hmm . . . They're probably all asleep," Vienna said. "Maybe we should leave them while they're being good," she suggested kindly.

"Okay," Mark replied, trying to hide his disappointment as he slowly made his way back to the living room.

"I bet I know what Mark wants for Christmas," Vienna commented, turning to Kit.

Kit made no response. She stood openmouthed, feeling much as if she'd been punched in the stomach. Mark's casual announcement that he, too, had been a "preemie" came as a total shock. Hadn't Nathan said he'd weighed in at over eight pounds? Something was definitely off kilter here.

Could Mark have been mistaken? But he would have no reason to lie. And if indeed he had been a "preemie," then it shed an entirely different light on the matter.

Kit tried to rein in her galloping thoughts. Was she mistaken about the figure Nathan used when he'd mentioned the child's birth weight? She didn't think so.

When she'd found Mark's birth certificate in Angela's safe-deposit box, Kit hadn't paid much attention to the baby's weight, it hadn't seemed important at the time. But now she wished she had.

"Kit! Is something wrong?" Vienna's voice cut through Kit's dazed thoughts, effectively bringing her back to the present.

"What? Oh, I'm sorry. I was daydreaming," she said, feeling embarrassed at her own rather rude behavior.

"You look like you've seen a ghost," Vienna said. "Are you sure you're all right?"

Kit summoned up a smile. "Yes, really. I'm fine," she assured Vienna who looked unconvinced.

"Need any help in here?" The question came from Drew who entered the kitchen and crossed to his wife. "Kade's asleep, finally."

"Good." His wife smiled up at him. "The dishes are all done," she said, reaching over to take the towel from Kit's unresisting fingers. "I'll get the rest later. Let's see how the tree looks."

The boys had done an admirable job trimming the tree and were duly praised for their decorating efforts. Though Kit tried to pretend nothing was amiss she found it impossible to stop thinking about what Mark had said and what it might mean.

She knew, too, that Nathan sensed something by the way he kept glancing over at her, and she wasn't surprised when a few minutes after nine he indicated that it was time to leave.

Kit hugged Vienna and thanked Tobias and Drew for a most memorable day, promising to pay a visit before she and Mark left for Vancouver and their return trip to England.

Mark fell asleep on the homeward journey and in the shadowed darkness of the van's interior Kit again tried to make sense of his earlier announcement.

Nathan brought the van to a halt in the driveway and after helping his mother to the front door and seeing her safely inside, he returned to the van to carry Mark into the house and upstairs to his room.

"We need to talk," Nathan said after he'd deposited Mark on top of his bed.

Kit nodded. "I'll come downstairs after I've put Mark to bed."

Mark awakened briefly as Kit undressed him, but made no protest as she tucked the blankets around him, mumbling sleepily something about his letter to Santa.

Kit paid a brief visit to her room, quickly locating the envelope she'd brought with her from England. Knowing Nathan would be waiting impatiently, she refrained from looking at the contents, wondering fleetingly what his reaction would be when she asked to see the copy of the birth certificate in his possession.

"Where's Joyce?" Kit asked him a few minutes later when she joined Nathan in the sitting room.

"She's rather tired. She went upstairs to her room. What happened at Vienna's? You looked upset about something. Why did you bring that?" he asked, noticing the envelope in her hand. "I told you I already had a copy."

Kit couldn't really blame him for being annoyed. "I think we should compare the birth certificate I brought with the copy you have," she explained.

"Why?" he asked, obviously puzzled by her request.

"Because of something Mark said earlier," Kit replied.

Nathan frowned. "I don't understand. What did Mark say?"

"It may be nothing at all," she responded. "But I think we should check it out."

"All right, it's in my desk upstairs. I'll be right back," Nathan said before making his way from the room.

Kit moved to stand in front of the gas fire, glad of its warmth. Her thoughts turned to Angela and Kit wondered anew at her friend's reasons for lying to Nathan, for wanting to deprive him of the child he'd fathered. Though Kit knew it was unlikely the real truth would ever be known, at the very least she might succeed in piecing some of it together.

"Here," Nathan said, tossing a white envelope onto the coffee table in front of her. "Now, would you kindly tell me what this is all about?"

Kit emptied the contents of her own envelope onto the table, then reached for the one Nathan had brought. Spreading both certificates in front of her, she quickly located the numbers she was seeking. On Nathan's copy of the birth certificate the baby's weight was cataloged as *eight pounds ten ounces* and on the certificate Kit had brought with her, the numbers read *three pounds ten ounces*.

Vienna had said Kade was born six weeks early and that his birth weight was almost five pounds. If Mark had weighed in at three pounds ten ounces, surely it was a strong indication that he, too, had been born prematurely, and definitely more than six weeks premature at that.

"Look at this," Kit said evenly, trying with difficulty to contain the excitement coursing through her.

"At what?" Nathan asked, obviously losing patience.

"Mark's birth weight on your copy is eight pounds ten ounces," she began evenly.

"Yes," Nathan agreed.

"The certificate I brought with me, which has to be the original because I found it in Angela's safe-deposit box after she died, doesn't match. Read the weight."

Nathan bent over the papers spread out on the table.

"Three pounds ten ounces . . . but that's not right," he said, glancing up at Kit, a puzzled expression on his face. "What the devil's going on here? That's a discrepancy of exactly five pounds."

He dropped his gaze to study the papers once more. "They look identical in every other respect," he noted. "Are you trying to tell me that someone tampered with this?"

Kit nodded. "Someone might have, if that someone was trying to prevent you from knowing the truth," Kit suggested.

"But Jamieson the private detective I hired to keep an eye on Angela, sent me this copy," Nathan said.

"What if Angela knew about Jamieson," Kit replied. "I didn't mention it before but that name sounded familiar to me. I'm sure I've seen it written somewhere among Angela's things." Kit was trying to work through the puzzle in a logical fashion. This could be the clue, the connection she'd been looking for.

Nathan ran a hand through his hair. "But if Angela had known about Jamieson—"

"And I'm positive she did," Kit cut in. "Wait a minute. I wonder..." She quickly flipped through the contents of the envelope she'd scattered on the table. Spotting a small address book that had belonged to Angela, Kit picked it up and as she did, something floated from between its pages to land on the table.

Nathan's hand snaked out to retrieve it. "Frank Jamieson, Private Detective, and his downtown Toronto address," he read aloud.

She hadn't been mistaken, thought Kit with a jolt. She must have seen the business card before and thought nothing more about it. But the simple fact that the detective's card was in Angela's possession could only mean one thing, Angela had to have known she was being watched.

"There's something written on the other side," Kit said noticing what looked like numbers scrawled there.

Nathan turned the card over. "A thousand dollars? What the blazes does that mean?"

Kit glanced at the figure written across the back of the card. "The fact that Angela had the card at all means she had to have known about the detective, known that he was following her," Kit proposed. "What exactly did you tell him when you hired him?" she asked.

Nathan gazed at her for a long moment. "I'm not sure just what instructions I gave him," he replied. "I think I told him that there was a possibility the child was mine, but I wouldn't know for sure until it was born."

"What if Jamieson saw a way to make more money for himself? What if he told Angela who'd hired him and why? Maybe they struck up a deal of some sort. Maybe that's what the thousand dollars written on the back of the card is all about."

Kit knew she was rambling, making wild guesses, but somehow as she voiced the outlandish notions she couldn't help wondering if she was closer to the truth than she knew.

"And by changing the birth weight to eight pounds ten ounces instead of the true weight of three pounds ten ounces, which would have indicated to me that the baby was premature and therefore quite probably mine. Angela cleverly and coldheartedly denied me my son," Nathan continued, anger threading his voice now.

He reached for the birth certificates once more, and though Kit saw the flash of anger in his eyes, there was also a glimmer of hope...of belief. "If all this speculating we're doing is in fact the truth—" Nathan broke off and turned to meet Kit's gaze.

"It would mean Mark really is your son...." she finished for him, emotion clogging her voice. "Why else would Angela have gone to all this trouble? It has to be true," Kit said, her heart filling with love for this man who'd obviously been tormented for so long. "Angela kept telling me she'd lied to you about everything. I suppose it was too much for her to try to explain...but she kept pleading with me to believe her, begging me to set the record straight."

Nathan dropped the papers onto the coffee table and clasped Kit's hands in his. "Then Mark really is my son?"

Kit felt tears prick at her eyes at the wonder she could hear in his voice. "Yes, he really is your son. Believe it. I do. That's why I came all this way. He's yours, your own flesh and blood," she assured him and as her eyes met his she thought she saw a glint of moisture in their depths only seconds before he hauled her into his arms.

"Thank you." His words were heartfelt and Kit merely sighed as she gave herself up to the joy of being in his arms. "There were times when I'd look at him and tell myself it was true, I wanted it to be true.... I can't begin to tell you what this means to me," he went on in a throaty whisper.

"Mark deserves a father like you and you deserve a son like him," Kit told him with love and sincerity.

Suddenly Nathan held her away from him. "I can't take it all in. Can you imagine how my mother will react when I tell her that she has a grandchild...she'll be ecstatic...over the moon. What a wonderful Christmas present for her. What a wonderful Christmas this is going to be." He was smiling now, his face a picture of happiness.

"I bet your mother's still awake. Why don't you go and tell her right now," Kit suggested, thinking Joyce deserved to hear the news.

"I think I will," Nathan said, releasing her and crossing to the door he disappeared from sight.

Kit stood for several moments staring after him. Slowly, inevitably, her feelings of joy began to drain away. She was happy for Mark, she truly was, she told herself. She'd accomplished what she'd set out to do: she'd united him with his real family.

But all at once she realized that with the success her role as his guardian was over, and though she loved Mark as if he were her own son, his rightful place was here, with his father and grandmother.

And while she knew that leaving Mark with his father would be difficult enough, walking away from Nathan, the man who'd come to mean everything to her, the man who'd stolen her heart, would be the hardest thing she'd ever had to do.

Chapter Thirteen

Kit gathered the papers scattered on the coffee table, thinking all the while that if Mark hadn't made that chance remark earlier, they would have returned to England without ever uncovering the truth.

Now she would be making that journey alone. Her hands stilled and she bit back the sob suddenly threatening to burst free. After all it wasn't as though she'd be leaving him with strangers, she reminded herself as she drew a steadying breath. A bond had already been established between Mark and his father, and the love and attention Mark would receive from both Nathan and Joyce would undoubtedly help him adjust to his new situation.

That Mark would be upset at her leaving was inevitable, and she would miss him, too, quite desperately. Since Angela's death he'd been the central focus of her life and one of the main reasons behind her decision to open up a photography studio of her own.

And that was a plan she didn't intend to abandon, she told herself resolutely. Once she returned to England she'd need something to occupy her waking hours, to help her forget, help her deal with the pain of not only leaving Mark with his father but leaving her own foolish heart with him as well.

Her thoughts shifted momentarily to the kiss they'd shared that afternoon. The kiss, though devoid of passion, had been overflowing with warmth, tenderness and understanding.

For her it had been a kiss of discovery, the kiss that had sealed her destiny; the kiss that had captured her soul. But when he'd ended the kiss abruptly, telling her it had been a mistake, he'd effectively crushed the faint stirrings of hope she'd had that he might also harbor feelings for her.

All that was left was an emptiness, an aching void she doubted she would ever be able to fill.

"Kit, my dear, Nathan just told me the news. Is it really true? Is Mark my grandson?" Joyce's excited voice cut through Kit's reverie and she quickly schooled her features before turning to face Mark's grandmother.

"Yes, it's true," Kit assured Joyce, careful to avoid looking at Nathan for fear he would see her distress.

"It's a miracle..." Joyce said, wiping away tears as she stopped in front of Kit. "I can hardly believe it...it's too wonderful." She was silent for a long moment and Kit reached out to gently squeeze her hand, managing only to nod in response, fighting to keep her own emotions in check.

"But there's something I don't understand," Joyce ventured, her gaze intent on Kit now. "Where do you fit in all this?"

Kit was relieved that there was neither hostility nor anger in Joyce's words, merely curiosity.

"Angela and I had been friends for a number of years," Kit explained and as she slowly recounted her connection with Angela and how she'd become involved in Mark's life, Joyce listened attentively, stopping her occasionally to ask a question.

"I can't tell you how much I admire you for taking the bull by the horns and bringing Mark here," Joyce said when Kit had finished. "It can't have been easy for you."

"I had to come. I had to try," Kit said, knowing that if she had to do it all again, she would.

Joyce turned to her son. "Mark reminded me of you when you were a boy...remember, I said that didn't I?" she asked, her smile widening.

"Several times," Nathan said with a shake of his head.

"What happens now?" Joyce queried. "Are there papers to sign...lawyers to meet..."

"I don't think that's necessary," Kit replied. "Mark's birth certificate names Nathan as his father, that's all the proof anyone including the authorities will need."

"But what about you, Kit? You love that child and he loves you," Joyce stated simply. "How are we going to explain all this to him? He's so young. How do we help him understand? He's going to need you."

Kit felt a lump rise in her throat and it was all she could do to answer. "Mark's a smart boy, a very smart boy," she replied softly. "My guess is that when we sit down with him and tell him the truth, he'll be thrilled. Didn't you hear him at Vienna's saying he wished he could stay forever? He's very attached to you and Nathan already. I'm sure he'll accept and adjust quickly," she said with more confidence than she felt. "All this excitement... and Christmas, too, he won't have time to think about me or even miss me, for that matter."

"Miss you?" Nathan repeated in a startled tone. "What do you mean, miss you? Where, exactly, are you planning on going?"

Kit turned to look at him. "Back to England, of course," she said, trying with difficulty to keep her voice even.

At her reply Nathan felt as if he'd been sideswiped by a speeding truck. He stood staring at Kit for several long moments digesting this information, and as the silence lengthened the tension in the room almost became tangible.

The sound of a car crunching to a halt in the snow outside broke the silence. "That must be Bruce and Carmen," Joyce said, relief in her tone.

Nathan turned to Joyce. "Why don't you go and meet them, Mother. Take them into the kitchen and tell them the news," he suggested. "I have a few details I want to sort out with Kit."

"Details? But, I thought—" Joyce began.

"Please, Mother," Nathan cut in, an edge to his voice that brooked no argument.

Joyce nodded and with a questioning glance at Kit, made her way from the room, closing the door behind her.

Kit bit back a sigh. She was at a loss to understand what details Nathan was talking about, but much as she wanted to go to her room, something in his demeanor, in the way he'd spoken kept her rooted to the spot.

Emotionally she felt drained and decidedly close to tears, but she was determined not to break down in front of him. She would do her grieving in private. After she'd said her good-byes.

"Just what are these details you're talking about?" she asked.

Nathan closed the gap between them, coming to a halt in front of her. "Just this..." he said, and before she could think or react, he pulled her into his arms and his mouth captured hers in a kiss that sent the world spinning crazily out of control.

Her lips tasted like the finest Cabernet only richer, darker, sensuous and much more exciting. Her response was open, honest, innocent, just like her, and yet there was an alluring, enticing, quality that tugged at his insides, sending a tremor through him that left him reeling.

He'd never before met a woman like her, a woman who knowing how much she had to lose, had still given so unselfishly. A woman who'd challenged him not only to relinquish his hold on the past, but move on and grab the future with both hands.

And that's exactly what he was doing, because in those moments when she'd spoken so casually of returning to England, he'd suddenly realized that the only future he wanted, the only future that he could envision for himself, was a future with her...and Mark...together, as a true family.

It didn't take a genius to figure out what had happened. Sometime during the past week she'd wound her way past his sleeping defenses, and captured his stubborn heart.

Oh, he'd fought his feelings at first, fearful as always of laying himself open to being hurt again. But it was a battle he'd had no chance of winning, because he'd fallen, deeply, unequivocally and quite desperately in love with her. He knew it now with a certainty that rocked him. But how did she feel about him? If her response was anything to go by, there might be hope for the best Christmas ever.

Kit was sure she was dreaming. Where else but in her dreams would Nathan kiss her with such passion, such hunger, igniting needs she'd never known before?

She willingly gave herself up to the fantasy, glorying in the sensations swirling through her, never wanting this to end. She moaned in frustration as her impatient hands foraged beneath his sweater until they were exploring the muscled contours of his back.

Her heart was beating a thunderous tattoo inside her breast, but she could feel another stronger rhythm throbbing insistently beneath her fingers.

Shock ricocheted through her and her heart skittered to a halt before gathering speed once more. She wasn't dreaming! This was real, incredibly, wonderfully real.

But why? The question dropped like a stray bomb into her mind, shattering both the dream and the reality into a thousand pieces.

It took every ounce of strength she had to break free of his kiss, and it was only a small consolation to note that Nathan appeared to be having as much difficulty catching his breath as she had.

"Aren't you going to tell me that this was just another *mistake*?" she asked, anger lacing her voice. "Perhaps disaster is a better word," she added, clinging by the tips of her fingers to what was left of her tattered composure.

"What?" Nathan asked, frowning in obvious puzzlement, and it was all she could do not to shake him.

Kit drew a ragged breath. "The last time you kissed me, you proceeded to tell me that it was a mistake," she said, her voice wavering fractionally.

Understanding dawned in his blue eyes, eyes still glittering with another emotion she couldn't quite decipher.

"Oh, but it was a mistake, you were—" Nathan began.

"Thank you, I'm glad you cleared that up." Pain sliced through her at his words.

"You didn't let me finish," Nathan said, a hint of exasperation in his voice now. "You were upset this afternoon and very vulnerable, you needed a friend, not a lover, and much as I wanted to make love with you, it was neither the time nor the place. Wooden floorboards and below zero temperatures aren't exactly my idea of comfort. When I make love with you I want everything to be perfect."

Kit could only stare in stunned silence at the man before her. Had he really said he wanted to make love with her? Her heart did a strange little hiccup inside her breast. "Are you trying to seduce me?" she asked.

"Most definitely," Nathan replied, his eyes alive with humor and something infinitely more alluring.

Kit wasn't quite sure if he was serious or not, she only knew that she didn't like games, at least not games like this, but before she could say anything Nathan continued.

"Do you really want to know why I kissed you just now?" he asked, gently capturing her chin in his hand and urging her to meet his gaze.

Kit tried to swallow the knot of emotion in her throat, but it wouldn't budge. "Yes...no, I don't know," she said in a husky whisper, mesmerized by the intensity in his eyes and the seductive sound of his voice.

"I kissed you because you are the most generous, loving, sensitive, caring woman I have ever met. Even knowing the price you might have had to pay, you still did what you thought was right and fought for what you believed in. You fought for the truth, and Mark and I were lucky to have had someone like you on our side."

Kit couldn't speak. Tears filled her eyes, and it was all she could do to stop them from overflowing. Though Nathan had so eloquently expressed his gratitude, the only trouble was, at this moment, she possessed few of the qualities he'd just described.

She was feeling selfish and greedy because she wanted more, more than she could ever hope for, more than he was willing to give... she wanted his love.

"You still don't get it, do you?" Nathan said with a sigh. "I'm going to have to spell it out..."

"Spell what out?" she asked, totally mystified.

Nathan gently put his hands on her shoulders. "Katherine Bellamy, you're not leaving. You're not going back to England. You're not going anywhere. Mark needs you now more than ever. This family needs you... but more importantly, I need you."

With his fingertip he tenderly wiped away the tear that had spilled down her cheek.

"You made me see how futile it was to dwell on the past. Angela and I were wrong for each other from the start. She saw it long before I did. I was just too stubborn to admit it. She tried to tell me, but I refused to listen and so she left. I felt angry, betrayed, but a part of me was also relieved and that brought on the guilt. It didn't take me long to realize that I'd never really been in love with her. I think we both made the mistake of falling in love with love."

As he spoke he began to unravel her hair from the braid she'd so carefully woven that morning. His fingers deftly combed it free, letting it fall like a silk curtain over her shoulders. Grabbing a handful he let it slide through his fingers.

"I can't really blame Angela for not wanting me to know about Mark," he continued in a sad tone. "I'll always have regrets about that:...but I can't change the past, I can only hope to shape the future...our future."

Nathan cradled her head in his hands and brought her face to within inches of his. "Don't you know that if you leave, there will be no future for me?" His voice was husky with emotion. "From the moment you came barging into my life I knew you were a force to be reckoned with, and I was right," he confessed, a faint smile tugging at his mouth. "I know how much you love my son. But would it be too much to hope for that there might be room in your heart for me?"

Kit felt her whole body tremble at his words. She could hear the vulnerability in his voice, see the apprehension in his eyes and she knew in that moment she'd never loved him more.

"What are you trying to say?" she asked in a breathless whisper, daring to hope, but desperate to hear the words that would make all her dreams come true.

Nathan smiled. "I love you," he said simply, truthfully and with heartfelt sincerity.

"I love you, too," she replied and almost before she'd finished speaking his mouth was on hers, instantly transporting them to their own private heaven.

It was several minutes before Nathan managed to tear himself away. He cradled her head in his hands, gazing into her eyes with a look of unbridled passion. "If we stay in here much longer with the door closed, my mother will think I'm seducing you," he said softly.

"She'd be right," Kit responded and lifted her mouth to brush the faint roughness of his jaw.

Nathan chuckled, a deep rumble of sound that sent her pulse skipping crazily. Kit put her ear to his chest and listened to the pounding of his heart, a beat that almost matched her own.

She drew away and looked up at the man who'd only minutes ago declared his love for her. "Maybe we'd better get out of here in case Santa decides to come down the chimney early," Kit said teasingly, thinking that Joyce and Carmen would indeed be wondering about them.

"Speaking of Santa," Nathan said turning her in his arms so that they stood looking at the Christmas tree, its lights twinkling merrily at them. "I think he'll have his work cut out for him in the next few days. But at least he knows where he can get his hands on a puppy a certain small boy has been asking for."

"Oh, Nathan." Kit blinked back the tears suddenly stinging her eyes and smiled up at him. "Mark will love it. Thank you. Oh, I can hardly wait for Christmas morning."

"Does that mean you're staying?" Nathan asked pulling her into his arms once more.

"For this Christmas and all the Christmases to come," Kit replied. "As long as Santa approves, of course," she added with a grin.

"Believe me, Santa would like nothing better than to make all your Christmas wishes come true," said Nathan as his mouth came down to claim hers once more.

*   *   *   *   *

HE'S MORE THAN
A MAN, HE'S
ONE OF OUR

REBEL DAD
Kristin Morgan

When Linc Rider discovered he was a father, he was determined to find his son and take him back. But he found that Eric already had a home with his adoptive mother, Jillian Fontenot. The choice wouldn't be easy: take the boy from such a beautiful, loving woman or leave his son behind. And soon it was too late to tell Jillian the real reason he'd spent so many days in her home—and in her arms....

Join Linc in his search for family—and love—in Kristin Morgan's REBEL DAD. Available in January—only from Silhouette Romance!

Fall in love with our **Fabulous Fathers!**

FF194

Take 4 bestselling love stories FREE

Plus get a FREE surprise gift!

UNDER THE MISTLETOE

*Where's the best place to find love
this holiday season?* UNDER THE MISTLETOE,
*of course! In this special collection, some of
your favorite authors celebrate the joy of the
season and the thrill of romance.*

Available in December from

Silhouette

ROMANCE™

SRXMAS

He staked his claim…

HONOR BOUND

by
New York Times
Bestselling Author

previously published under the pseudonym Erin St. Claire

As Aislinn Andrews opened her mouth to scream, a hard
hand clamped over her face and she found herself face-
to-face with Lucas Greywolf, a lean, lethal-looking
Navajo and escaped convict who swore he wouldn't hurt
her— *if* she helped him.

Look for HONOR BOUND at your favorite
retail outlet this January.

Only from…

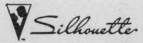

Share in the joys of finding happiness and exchanging the
ultimate gift—love—in full-length classic holiday
treasures by two bestselling authors

JOAN HOHL
EMILIE RICHARDS

Available in December at
your favorite retail outlet.

Only from 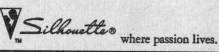 where passion lives.

Silhouette Books
is proud to present
our best authors,
their best books...
and the best in
your reading pleasure!

Throughout 1993, look for exciting
books by these top names in
contemporary romance:

DIANA PALMER—
The Australian in October

FERN MICHAELS—
Sea Gypsy in October

ELIZABETH LOWELL—
Chain Lightning in November

CATHERINE COULTER—
The Aristocrat in December

JOAN HOHL—
Texas Gold in December

LINDA HOWARD—
Tears of the Renegade in January '94

When it comes to passion,
we wrote the book.

BOBT3

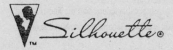

**Fifty red-blooded, white-hot, true-blue hunks
from every State in the Union!**

Look for MEN MADE IN AMERICA! Written by some
of our most poplar authors, these stories feature fifty of
the strongest, sexiest men, each from a different state in
the union!

Two titles available every other month at your favorite
retail outlet.

In January, look for:

DREAM COME TRUE by Ann Major (Florida)
WAY OF THE WILLOW by Linda Shaw (Georgia)

In March, look for:

TANGLED LIES by Anne Stuart (Hawaii)
ROGUE'S VALLEY by Kathleen Creighton (Idaho)

You won't be able to resist MEN MADE IN AMERICA!

SILHOUETTE.... Where Passion Lives

Don't miss these Silhouette favorites by some of our most popular authors!
And now, you can receive a discount by ordering two or more titles!

Silhouette Desire®

#05751	THE MAN WITH THE MIDNIGHT EYES BJ James	$2.89	☐
#05763	THE COWBOY Cait London	$2.89	☐
#05774	TENNESSEE WALTZ Jackie Merritt	$2.89	☐
#05779	THE RANCHER AND THE RUNAWAY BRIDE Joan Johnston	$2.89	☐

Silhouette Intimate Moments®

#07417	WOLF AND THE ANGEL Kathleen Creighton	$3.29	☐
#07480	DIAMOND WILLOW Kathleen Eagle	$3.39	☐
#07486	MEMORIES OF LAURA Marilyn Pappano	$3.39	☐
#07493	QUINN EISLEY'S WAR Patricia Gardner Evans	$3.39	☐

Silhouette Shadows®

#27003	STRANGER IN THE MIST Lee Karr	$3.50	☐
#27007	FLASHBACK Terri Herrington	$3.50	☐
#27009	BREAK THE NIGHT Anne Stuart	$3.50	☐
#27012	DARK ENCHANTMENT Jane Toombs	$3.50	☐

Silhouette Special Edition®

#09754	THERE AND NOW Linda Lael Miller	$3.39	☐
#09770	FATHER: UNKNOWN Andrea Edwards	$3.39	☐
#09791	THE CAT THAT LIVED ON PARK AVENUE Tracy Sinclair	$3.39	☐
#09811	HE'S THE RICH BOY Lisa Jackson	$3.39	☐

Silhouette Romance®

#08893	LETTERS FROM HOME Toni Collins	$2.69	☐
#08915	NEW YEAR'S BABY Stella Bagwell	$2.69	☐
#08927	THE PURSUIT OF HAPPINESS Anne Peters	$2.69	☐
#08952	INSTANT FATHER Lucy Gordon	$2.75	☐

	AMOUNT	$ _____
DEDUCT:	10% DISCOUNT FOR 2+ BOOKS	$ _____
	POSTAGE & HANDLING	$ _____
	($1.00 for one book, 50¢ for each additional)	
	APPLICABLE TAXES*	$ _____
	TOTAL PAYABLE	$ _____
	(check or money order—please do not send cash)	

To order, complete this form and send it, along with a check or money order for the
total above, payable to Silhouette Books, to: *In the U.S.*: 3010 Walden Avenue,
P.O. Box 9077, Buffalo, NY 14269-9077; *In Canada*: P.O. Box 636, Fort Erie, Ontario,
L2A 5X3.

Name: _____

Address: _____ City: _____

State/Prov.: _____ Zip/Postal Code: _____

*New York residents remit applicable sales taxes.
Canadian residents remit applicable GST and provincial taxes.

SBACK-OD

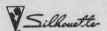